THE EMPEROR

THE EMPEROR

BY

H. ALBERTUS BOLI

PITTSBURGH

DR. BOLI'S CELEBRATED
PUBLISHING EMPIRE

2022

CHAPTER 1

THE SULTAN'S COLLECTION

GREAT and magnificent is the city on the Narrows, and great and magnificent is the palace of the sultan in the middle of it, and great and magnificent, as a matter of course, is everything within that palace; but the thing that gives the Sultan the most pleasure, and the thing he is most likely to invite a distinguished guest to inspect, is his collection. The Sultan collects rare, beautiful, and exquisite things. It is true that everything in his possession merits that description to some degree: he has a number of rare, beautiful, and exquisite wives, and his palace is decorated with the rarest, most beautiful, and most exquisite works of art from every country and every age. But there are some things so rare, so beautiful, and so exquisite that they are kept in a separate wing of the palace, virtually a palace of its own.

Important visitors—and it is a principle of the Sultan's hospitality that every visitor is important—are invariably asked whether they would like to see this collection; and since they have been warned beforehand that an affirmative answer would be wise (for the Sultan's ministers like it best when the Sultan is happy with his guests and there is no mess to clean up afterwards), they invariably accept his invitation.

So it happened when the Maharajah of Istanistan and his retinue paid a visit to the Sultan some time ago: the party adjourned from the immense dining hall after a particularly lavish feast and made its way through passages that were half corridor and half garden toward the collection rooms, as dozens of other parties of guests had done on dozens of other occasions. On this occasion, however, the Sultan's ministers observed a few signs of uncertainty in their master. The signs were invisible to all but those who had known the Sultan for most of his life, but they were there: a smile (or at least a width of mustache) just a little too broad, a voice just half a step too high, a slight syncopation in his normally regular rolling gait. And the ministers knew the reason for these signs: the Maharajah was also a collector, and his collection was said to rival the Sultan's. Since the Maharajah was an equal and a carefully cultivated ally, there could be no question of adding his head to the Sultan's collection. But someone would suffer if the Maharajah proved insufficiently impressed. The Sultan's ministers were worried.

Their worries did not diminish as the Maharajah was introduced to some of the glories of the collection. The Maharajah was scrupulously polite: he greeted every object with a bland smile and a few appropriate words of appreciation, always adding the disturbing information that he possessed something very similar.

"The head of Prometheus by Archippus," the Sultan announced, looking up at his guest to judge his reaction. The Sultan was a naturally small man, though the constant attention of the best cooks in his domain had rounded him into a sphere. "It is all that remains of his colossal Prometheus Bound, mentioned with such admiration by Pliny."

"Yes, very fine indeed," the Maharajah replied after a cursory examination of the huge head, which was a good bit taller than he was—and the Maharajah was a tall man, whose natural taste for asceticism had given him the appearance of one of those spindly pillars that formed thick forests in many parts of the Sultan's palace. He looked down at the Sultan, but he might have seemed to be looking not so much at his host as at his own reflection in the Sultan's perfectly oiled helmet of black hair. "I have his Ariadne. A remarkable composition—perfectly intact, of course."

There was a slight twitch in the Sultan's upper lip: it might have passed entirely unnoticed had not his immense and luxuriant black mustache amplified the movement, so that by the time it reached the ends the mustache seemed to be trying to fly away like a raven. Nevertheless, the Sultan proceeded with what was probably a smile to the next item, a water organ that played, by an ingenious arrangement of cams on a wheel, a simple but very loud melody without the intervention of a human musician. The Sultan's ministers discreetly stopped their ears, and the Maharajah's party listened with petrified smiles; but the Maharajah himself maintained his cheerful blandness throughout the brief performance.

When the tootling ended and the mechanism hissed and clattered to a stop, the Maharajah rendered his appreciation: "Very elegantly constructed. Mine plays "The Lament of the Amazons.'"

In their minds some of the Sultan's lesser ministers began to consider how they might formulate their wills.

So it was with most of the exhibits. The Maharajah pronounced the brazen oak with singing silver birds quite lovely: his own had birds made of gold, but the same mechanical principles were employed. The crystal tank with live sea-elephant was quite fascinating in its way: the Maharajah could offer some helpful advice on feeding the creature, based on his own success in keeping a breeding colony of the things.

With each successive exhibit the Sultan seemed less confident to his experienced ministers, who in turn were losing confidence in the attachment of their own heads to their bodies.

But the Sultan had not finished yet. "My dear Maharajah," he said at last, "surely your collection must be one of the wonders of the world, and in almost every way the equal of my own. There remains, however, one thing in my collection that is unique, a precious treasure so rare and exquisite that I must keep it separately. Would you like to have a glimpse of it?"

"My dear Sultan," the Maharajah replied, "nothing would please me more."

CHAPTER 2

A PRISONER OF HIS PERCEPTIONS

FROM the Stoa there is a magnificent view across the Narrows to the Sultan's palace and the city surrounding it, with its hills built over as far as the eye can see. It is a fine place to enjoy a quiet conversation, and the Emperor was wont to take his lessons there when the weather co-operated. On a particularly fine day some time ago, the young Emperor—he had not long previously endured the celebrations of his twenty-second birthday—was sitting with Iamblichus the philosophy tutor and making some half-hearted attempt to listen to him.

The scent of the sea was wonderfully invigorating. The sounds of the waves and the gulls, the shimmering glare on the water, the vast prospect of the city across the Nar-rows—they all made the Emperor feel alive, awake, and alert. They all made a philosophy lesson with Iamblichus endurable.

What had Iamblichus just said? The Emperor re-peated it in his mind: "That a world exists beyond our-selves cannot be demonstrated." It sounded silly.

"I see it right there," the Emperor replied with an expansive gesture that took in the whole view from the Stoa.

"Ah! But you have seen things in dreams, have you not?" the old philosopher asked. "And yet, on waking, you determined that they did not exist."

"But I can feel the wind, and smell the sea, and hear the gulls."

"As you might do in a dream. You have perceptions: that much you know."

"And I know that I'm perceiving the world with them. Don't I?"

"That," replied the philosopher with one of those subtly superior smiles of his—"That is the very question that cannot be answered."

"Where else would my perceptions come from?"

"Perhaps from your mind. Perhaps only your mind exists, and there is nothing else."

"Then who are you?"

Iamblichus' smile shifted slightly, from superior to tolerant. "I may be only a figure in the dream that is your life."

"Do you feel like a figure in my dream?"

"Ah, but you see you may be only a figure in my dream."

"You can't believe that, or you wouldn't be talking to me."

"Why not?" Now Iamblichus' face took on that slightly distant expression that indicated he was going to do some serious expounding. "Whether the world exists outside of me or only in my perceptions, the effect is the same from my point of view. I avoid perceptions that are unpleasant, and seek out perceptions that are pleasant. It makes no difference to me whether those perceptions correspond to realities in the external world. It may be so, or my life may be a long dream, or it may all be an elaborate pageant composed for my entertainment by powers beyond my knowledge. I know only what I perceive, and whether an external world exists cannot be demonstrated one way or another."

"You mean I'm a prisoner of my perceptions?"

"You might put it that way. Yes, that is very succinct, and rather clever."

The Emperor turned and gazed out across the Narrows again. He watched a cormorant vanish under the water; then his eye drifted upward to the towers and palaces and huddled crowds of houses of the city across the strait. A movement caught his eye: the cormorant had surfaced again, only its head and neck bobbing above the gentle swells.

"So if I threw you in the sea," he said without looking back at Iamblichus, "you would only *perceive* that you were wet?"

"Perhaps," Iamblichus replied.

"How long would it take you to perceive that you had drowned?"

There was a moment of silence, filled only by the sounds of the sea and the gulls; then Iamblichus said, "I believe it is nearly time for your daily audience."

Meanwhile, in the cool shadows down below the Stoa, in the corner formed by the intersection of the Dome with the seaward wall of the palace complex, two very respectable gentlemen had been listening to the Emperor's philosophy lesson.

"Is it wise," asked the Tribune, "to allow Iamblichus

to stuff his head with so much speculation?" He spoke in what was for him a low voice, but the other gentleman— an older, larger, and in every way more substantial figure —raised one finger to indicate that speech was not yet called for.

They waited for some time, the lesser figure hardly breathing while that finger remained in the air, as the Emperor went his way back into the palace. At last the finger subsided, and the elder man spoke.

"It is the very best thing for him," the Consul explained with calm assurance. "While his mind is on abstractions, he is not bothered with the concrete. When he does not meddle with the concrete, he is no danger to us."

"But what Iamblichus said was—"

"Abstract nonsense, my dear Tribune. The sort of thing philosophers are known for. Philosophy is just the thing for our young emperor—philosophy, and plenty of it. Let him spend his whole day looking for the *eidos* of a table if he likes: it will keep him from asking about the table itself."

"Is there something wrong with the table?" asked the lesser man.

"I chose the table as a representative example. I mean to say that I prefer his thoughts to linger in the ideal world, so that he does not think thoughts that might cost us our heads. I am very much attached to my head."

"But the Sultan—"

The finger came up again, producing another burst of silence. When, after some time, the finger was gradually lowered, its owner resumed in a lower voice:

"We do not speak that name."

The smaller man breathed again and nodded, and the two of them retired from the scene in silence.

CHAPTER 3

THE HALL OF LIONS

GUARDS whose only function was to open the pair of great doors opened the pair of great doors, the doors adorned with tremendous reliefs of lions by a great ancient sculptor so great and so ancient that his name had been forgotten for centuries. The doors, as high as four men standing on one another's shoulders, opened slowly, and with many groans from their hidden parts and an occasional sudden report of clanging popping bronze. Their slowness was part of the ceremony, and any entry into the Hall of Lions was by definition ceremonial.

Their heads bowed, the Consul and the Tribune waited until the doors had stopped moving; then they stepped through the doorway, their eyes still on their feet and on the wonderfully lifelike mosaic pictures of lions on the floor—lions at rest, lions prowling, lions chasing their prey, lions being hunted by long-dead Emperors of the distant and glorious past. If they had turned their eyes to the left or to the right, the two men might have surveyed, across the vast expanse of floor and behind the lines of guards in their best ceremonial dress, the colossal reliefs of lions along the walls, reliefs picked out in gold leaf against a background of imperial purple mellowed by immemorial age. But they did not look to the left or to the right, since they walked through the Hall of Lions every day and were immune to its impressive decorations. And they certainly did not look ahead of them. That was *not permitted*—not until the lion had roared. Above all things, the etiquette of the imperial court must be respected and preserved.

The two men walked in step, in spite of a significant difference in the length of their legs: they had walked together so often and so long that matching their strides came naturally to them. They slowed in step as they neared the imperial dais, and they stopped on the same foot, as always, just in front of the mosaic of the Emperor Adrianus XVII wearing the skin of the lion he had slain in the previous mosaic. And there they stood, looking down at their feet, while the Emperor sat on the throne in his itchy purple robe, the sword of Adrianus XXI in his right hand, and the long lines of guards stood against the walls and stared at the guards on the other side of the vast hall, and no one glanced toward the throne, because no one might look at the Emperor until the lion had roared.

Then there was a sound of whirring and accelerating clicking, and the clacking and creaking and clanking of bronze moving against bronze, and one of the life-size bronze lions, the one to the Emperor's right, began to rise ponderously on its haunches. It rose slowly, and its forelegs had just begun to lift from the ground, when the clicking slowed, and the whirring came to a halt, and there was silence.

The Consul and the Tribune stared at their feet. The

Emperor stared at the tops of their heads.

Still there was silence.

After rather too much silence, the Emperor made a loud "Pssst!" sound, and whispered in a harsh hiss, "The thump!"

The Master of the Beasts, standing until that moment to one side of the imperial dais, now stepped up to the half-standing bronze lion and gave it a resounding whack with the flat of his palm. The loud hollow clang was followed by a resumption of the whirring and clicking, and the lion rose to stand on its hind legs with much creaking, until at last it emitted a very convincing if slightly tinny roar.

On that signal, the soldiers along the walls turned to face the Emperor, and the Consul and the Tribune looked up in time to see the bronze lion subside into its usual resting position.

"The Emperor's compliments to the Senate and the People," the Emperor said in his best imperial voice.

The Consul replied, "The greetings of the Senate to the Emperor, the bearer of their burdens."

The Tribune added, "The greetings of the People to the Emperor, the guardian of their rights."

Now that the required formalities had been observed, the Emperor visibly relaxed on his throne, with a few slightly awkward movements that might help relieve the itching without actually scratching, which was not done in the Hall of Lions.

"Well," he said, "what is the business of the day? Corruption in the provinces? The war in Aspersia?"

"A diplomatic matter, your clemency," said the Consul. "A suitable gift must be found for the Sultan's collection."

"Oh, yes—I suppose that is important," the Emperor said, though "important" would not have been the first word that occurred to him to describe it.

"Very much so," said the Tribune, glancing up at the Consul.

"The Sultan," said the Consul, "is a useful—I might say essential—vassal and ally, and it behooves us to treat him well."

"And," the Tribune added, "the Sultan will also soon be your father-in-law."

"Yes, in ten years," said the Emperor.

"Nine," the Consul corrected him. "His daughter will be sixteen in nine years."

"I'm sure it will be worth the wait," the Emperor said, though without any marks of strong conviction. "And how is my beloved Spring Flower After the... the... Storm?"

"Spring Blossom After the Rain, your clemency," the Consul said. "The Sultan takes pride in giving all his daughters poetic names, and it might be well to make an effort to memorize the name of your betrothed, especially since the Sultan took the trouble to conceive her just for you."

"I hope it wasn't too *much* trouble," the Emperor mumbled.

"Oh, I don't think so," the Tribune said. "He had, what, thirty-seven daughters before her, and dozens after, so it must be no trouble at all." At that moment, rather too late, the Tribune glanced up at the Consul and saw his expression.

"As to your inquiry," the Consul continued, "we are informed that Spring Blossom After the Rain is in perfect health, and as beautiful as her name implies."

"Oh, good," the Emperor said. "Glad to hear it. That's good, then. She's progressing... well."

"And since you have brought it up, it would be very wise and considerate to send a gift for Spring Blossom After the Rain along with the gift for her father—some appropriate expression of devotion for your betrothed."

"Yes, I'm sure," the Emperor said. "What do you suppose would be an appropriately devoted gift for a seven-year-old girl?"

"Jewels are always appropriate and appreciated," the Consul replied. "Anticipating your clemency's desires, we took the liberty of asking the Master of the Treasury to search the collections for a suitable token." Suddenly his voice was much louder: "The Master of the Treasury!"

Down the row of guards along the wall to the Emperor's right, the tenth guard shouted, "The Master of the Treasury!" And then the twentieth guard in the left-hand row shouted, "The Master of the Treasury!" And the thirtieth guard in the right-hand row shouted, "The Master of the Treasury!"

A large silver tray with velvet lining entered the back of the hall, with a little grey-headed man behind it. As the tray came nearer—which, in a hall that was two hundred imperial cubits from front to back, continued to happen for some time—the Emperor could see that it appeared to be piled with jewels.

At last the little man reached the foot of the imperial dais, and with some effort he lifted the tray to the Consul's level.

The Consul took hold of a gold chain, and the whole pile of gems and filigree came with it, revealing itself as one ponderous necklace crusty with precious stones and terminating in an immense carbuncle.

"It belonged to the Empress Eudoxia the Great," the Consul said. "She wore it when she received the submission of the King of Aspersia."

"It's impressive," the Emperor remarked. "But isn't it a bit weighty or a seven-year-old girl?"

"She'll grow into it," said the Tribune.

The Emperor shrugged, causing the Consul to wince, and the Emperor to remember the Consul's lecture on the subject of unimperial gestures. "That's settled, then. We have a gift for Spring Blossom After the... Rain?" The Consul nodded, and the Emperor continued: "So now we have only the Sultan to consider. What did we give him last year?"

"Irene," said the Consul.

"Irene?"

"His fifty-ninth wife," the Tribune explained.

"Oh, yes, I remember. I don't suppose it would do to give him a wife two years in a row. It would be monotonous."

"Indeed," said the Consul.

"Have you any suggestions, then?"

Clearly the Consul and the Tribune had been waiting for this question. "In fact,"said the Consul, "we have thought of something—not a gift per se, but a way of finding a suitable gift."

"Oh, I'm glad to hear it. What's your plan?"

The Consul happily explained. "We are blessed in the

palace and its dependencies with some of the most skillful craftsmen in the Empire. Let the guilds be told that each is to present one splendid example of its art, and that the very most splendid will be presented to the Sultan. The result, I am sure, will be at least one gift worthy of the Sultan's collection, something rare and exquisite and unique in the world."

"Good idea," the Emperor said. "And who judges which one is the best?"

"Your clemency will be the judge, of course," said the Tribune.

"With our advice, of course," the Consul added. It really went without saying, because the Emperor had always done everything with the advice of the Consul and the Tribune, ever since he had been a tiny little Emperor who could hardly sit up in the throne by himself.

So the great business of the day was settled: a committee consisting of the heads of the guilds, with the Tribune as its chairman, would establish the details of the great contest, and the entries would be presented to the Emperor for his judgment. As always, the Emperor reached his decision very easily, because the decision appeared to have been made beforehand, and presented to him in such a way that he had only to approve what was obviously reasonable.

"Are we finished, then?" the Emperor asked.

"If your clemency has no other business to discuss," the Consul replied.

"Then the Emperor thanks the Senate and the People for their confidence," said the Emperor.

"The Senate thanks the Emperor for the burden of government he bears," said the Consul.

"The People thank the Emperor for his protection," said the Tribune.

This little ceremony ended the audience, and the two lines of guards, along with the Master of the Beasts, the Master of the Treasury, and a few other assorted Masters whose presence had been requested but not made use of, filed out the exit between the immense lion doors.

They had not finished filing before the Emperor grasped his purple robe and pulled it over his head, getting himself stuck in it for a moment, and then triumphantly escaped from it and tossed it behind him. A servant who had been hovering invisibly in the way of all good servants—a little round man with slick black hair and an immense black mustache—appeared in the background and scooped up the robe, then carried it off with a peculiar rolling gait.

"That thing itches," the Emperor declared, smoothing out his white robe and the tunic underneath. "No matter how many layers I wear under it, it still itches."

"That robe was worn by Adrianus XIII," the Consul said with an expression of severe disapproval.

"He probably hated it as much as I do. Can't we find something else?"

The Consul smiled the smile of a father whose child is throwing a rather amusing tantrum. "It is necessary to keep up the traditions of the imperial court."

"Even when the traditions are itchy?"

"Especially when the traditions are itchy."

The Emperor tried to think of something to say in reply, but there was really nothing to be said. Of course the Consul was right, because "the Consul is right" had been the first principle of his imperial training.

"Well," the Emperor said at last, "I'd like to take a walk along the Colonnade. The sea air will do me good."

"It will be our pleasure to accompany you," said the Consul.

"Do you think, just this once, I might go by myself?"

"It will be our pleasure to accompany you," the Consul repeated with an iron smile.

CHAPTER 4

THE GREAT COLONNADE

SURELY nothing like the Great Colonnade adorns any other palace in the world. It runs for more than half an imperial mile in a gentle curve along the shore of the Sea of Aspersia, a shore that has been carefully molded and regularized to form a perfect arc. The Colonnade begins at the Dome, and the lines of perfectly fluted Ionic columns on either side of the promenade support a gleaming marble roof that almost seems to glow from within. Occasionally one can detect a scrap of color in the volutes or the moldings, betraying the gaudier tastes of a long-past age, when even the finest marble was gaily painted in brilliant polychrome; but now there is nothing but the white of the marble to meet the eye as the Colonnade runs along beside the Hall of Lions and curves in front of the imperial residential quarters, and then past three ancient temples now turned into a church and two residences for clergy, until at last it terminates in a round lookout at the point of land where the Sea of Aspersia meets the Gulf of the Heptapolis.

Here the Emperor loved to stroll and gaze out to sea and imagine far-off places; and he would have enjoyed it even more if he had been able to stroll by himself and think uninterrupted thoughts, but of course that was not possible. The Emperor was never by himself. It was not done, and that was the end of it.

"A yellow sail!" the Emperor called out, pointing with undisguised glee. He sometimes looked very much like a little boy when something like this took hold of his imagination.

"Yes," the Tribune said, "the yellow sail of—"

"Of Cnaedus," the Emperor filled in, interrupting him, "the richest port in the Heptapolis. It must be on its way to the spice colonies of the South with a load of fine dyed linens to trade for pepper and cinnamon and cloves. You see, I did pay attention to my geography lessons."

"And a very good thing," said the Consul. "A knowledge of geography has already served you well in the administration of your Empire, and will continue to be of service in the years to come."

"Don't you think, though," asked the Emperor, "that there are better ways to learn about the world than geography lessons?"

"'What do you mean?" asked the Consul suspiciously.

"I mean I know the chief products of the cities of the Heptapolis. I can name the most famous churches and palaces. I can tell you that Scythians are the best horsemen in the world, and I can describe the camps of the nomads in Nabatea, I know the names of the islands great and small in the Sea of Aspersia, and I can name the chief trading posts around the Northeast Sea beyond the Narrows. But I've never seen any of those things. Some day I'd like to. I think it would help me as Emperor, don't you?"

"No," said the Consul and the Tribune together.

"But how can I make wise decisions about provinces I haven't seen?" the Emperor asked. "If I knew the people and the places—"

"The way it is done," the Consul explained, "is that the Emperor is presented with all the information that is relevant to his decision."

"And then, of course," the Tribune added, "his most trusted advisors give him the guidance necessary to make the correct decision."

"Of course," the Consul agreed. "An excessively detailed knowledge of the provinces would only hinder you in making correct decisions."

The Emperor sighed and gazed across the water at that billowing yellow sail. An ordinary sailor, a man of no family, with nothing to his name but the clothes on his back, was free to sail to the spice colonies whenever the notion struck him. But it was forbidden to an Emperor.

"I still think it would be good for me to travel," the Emperor said quietly.

"That is not done," the Consul said with one of his very firm smiles.

"Besides," added the Tribune, "the rest of the world can hardly compare with the palace."

"'That is true," the Consul quickly agreed. "There may be famous churches, but what could compare for sheer magnificence with our own Church of the Assumption? The markets of Cnaedus may be famous, but the very best of all the world's exports can be found in our own Forum."

"And the Dome is famous all over the world," the Tribune remarked.

"Surely the Hanging Gardens of Babylon could hardly equal our Terrace Garden," said the Consul (though here the Emperor privately accused him of some exaggeration). "And where else is there a theater with the Pool of St. Tryphaena for a backdrop?" (To this the Emperor could make no objection, since in all his geographical studies he had heard of no other Pool of St. Tryphaena than the one on the grounds of the palace.)

"And the Pharos of Cynopsis is three cubits shorter than the Tower of Diotrephes," said the Tribune, apparently eager to show that his own geographical education had not been neglected.

"So you see," the Consul concluded, "there is really nothing to be seen in the rest of the world that cannot be seen better here in the palace. The palace is a perfect miniature of the world in itself: it is the world in epitome."

The Emperor was silent, watching the yellow sail as it dwindled toward the horizon.

The Tribune felt moved to add, "The Fountain Court is nice, too." But receiving no response, he fell silent as well.

For a quarter of an hour or so the three ambled along mostly in silence, one or another of them remarking every so often on a gull or a cormorant or a dolphin, so as to keep the silence from growing to an unbearable weight. At last they reached the end of the Great Colonnade, where it widened into a broad circular pavilion with a marble bench all the way around the perimeter. Here the Emperor sat and turned to face the sea, imagining all the places it might take him if he were only a common man and not the embodiment of empire. To his left was the

Sea of Aspersia, which connected with the illimitable ocean, from which an ambitious sailor might reach any port in the world. To his right was the Gulf of the Heptapolis, bordered by seven legendary cities whose marine trade had brought them the treasures of all nations. Would he never see any of them? And there was the sea itself, whose depths held mysteries hardly even imagined by the philosophers, but familiar to every common sailor. The Emperor's only experience with the nautical life was an occasional excursion across the pool of St. Tryphaena on a small barge, and even that indulgence was rarely permitted him. He glanced down at the imperial-purple border of his white robe, and it seemed to him—not for the first time—that it was a border between worlds, a line of demarcation that he was forbidden to cross.

"Well," the Emperor said in a lazily indifferent tone, "I think I might as well go back."

Suddenly he leaped from his seat and started to run back along the promenade as fast as his legs would carry him, lifting his robes with one hand. It had taken the Consul and the Tribune completely by surprise: they were far behind him, shouting things he didn't care to hear. And as the Emperor ran, a very wicked thought came to him: he might leave the promenade altogether and dash unaccompanied into the vast grounds of the palace, which was a substantial city in its own right; he might even, if he dared, go through the gate and explore for the first time the city beyond the wall.

But that did not happen. At the first exit from the promenade, the one by St. Sosipater's, there were two guards standing in the way, not in a threatening manner but simply in an immobile manner. So the Emperor ran on, impelled by a gleeful sense of naughtiness he hadn't felt for a long time. He considered leaping over the rail, but it was six feet to the ground, and there were roses all along the landward side—very sweet and very thorny. So he followed his original plan, which was no plan at all: he simply ran and ran until he reached the Dome, and then he stopped, panting and laughing, and waited quite a while for the Consul and the Tribune to catch up with him.

When they did they were panting but not laughing. They scolded him in that gentle and delicate way they had—using phrases like "perhaps not advisable"—that usually made him feel ashamed of himself. But this time he felt too euphoric to be properly ashamed. And his euphoria only increased when he reminded himself that the moon would be nearly full that night. When the sky was clear and the moon was bright, he could enter his own world—a world even the Consul and the Tribune knew nothing about.

The rest of the day passed in dull routine fashion. There was a dancing lesson in the Dome, whose immense hollow emptiness made it hard to hear what his dancing-master was telling him. But there was no need for him to hear. Dancing for an Emperor consisted entirely of moving one's feet in one of a small number of prescribed patterns while keeping the rest of one's body as rigid as possible; and doubtless the dancing-master was only saying that he ought to do it with more grace, which was absurd if he was supposed to remain as expressionless as a marble statue. And then came dinner, which consisted of a number of different very expensive meats and fishes, expertly prepared so that no disturbingly intense flavors would ever assault the imperial tongue. The dinner was also attended by a few important persons who had been granted the inestimable privilege of dining with the Emperor, though what good it did them he could never tell, since they scrupulously avoided mentioning anything that might give him a hint as to why they were important.

At last, after some improving reading carefully chosen for the Emperor by the Master of the Library, it was time to end the day. The Emperor retired to his vast bedchamber, just a few paces from the Hall of Lions; he was dressed by imperial valets in his imperial nightclothes (they were nearly indistinguishable from his day clothes, but somehow more nocturnal, and it would never do to sleep in his day clothes), and he settled down among the pillows in his immense bed while soft music played to lull him to sleep.

The Emperor hated the soft music.

It was not that he hated music;—quite the reverse. He paid close attention to the music. He loved music, and it occupied his mind so much that, no matter how soft the harp or sweet the rebec, he could not sleep until the music had stopped. And that posed a difficulty, because the musicians were not allowed to stop until the Emperor had gone to sleep. On more than one occasion he had suggested very gently that the musicians might be dispensed with, just for a night or two, so that he could be alone with his silent thoughts as he drifted off to sleep; but these suggestions met with gentle but immovable resistance. The best musicians in the palace had trained all their lives in the hope of being invited to join the imperial bedchamber orchestra. Would he deprive them of the one privilege to which they had devoted their entire existence?

In the end, the Emperor found that it was best to let the musicians lull him to sleep. He did not really sleep, of course. The music kept him awake, as music always did. But he got to be very good at feigning sleep. He did not snore ostentatiously: that would not have fooled the Master of the Emperor's Music, or worse it might have earned him an appointment with the imperial physician, who would prescribe a remedy for snoring that would taste absolutely foul, since it was the imperial physician's firm belief that the efficacy of the remedy was indicated by its degree of foulness. No: the Emperor learned to slow his breathing down, to close his throat just a bit to make an audible restriction of the air flow, and to lie quite still, but with a few slight twitches at appropriate moments to indicate that he had passed into the world of dreams. In the almost-dark room, illuminated only by a small lamp in the corner near the musicians and, on those nights when the moon shone bright, the moonbeams through the immense window that overlooked the Sea of Aspersia through the Great Colonnade, the Emperor's performance was very effective.

And it would have to be especially effective tonight, because the Emperor had plans for the moonlight, and sleeping was not among them.

The rebec player was really inspired tonight, and it was almost a shame to cut his performance short. But it had to be done. The Emperor knew better than to mimic sleep right away: he gave the musicians about a quarter-hour of apparent wakefulness before he began to slow his breathing. Soon it was time for his first twitch, which was managed very artistically; then he added a bit of a rasp to his breathing. And then the Master of the Emperor's Music padded to the side of the emperor's bed in his velvet-soled slippers (which were meant to be utterly silent, but made a kind of very soft crushing sound when they reached the thick carpets that surrounded the imperial bed). Here was where the performance had to be completely perfect. The eyes could not open; the breathing could not change. Patience was essential. The Emperor managed it without any difficulty. He heard the velvet footsteps retreating; the music stopped; the musicians almost (but not quite) silently packed up their instruments and left the room; the great door closed without the least creak from its perfectly fitted hinges. There was no sound now but the gentle lapping of the waves on the other side of the Great Colonnade.

The Emperor lay motionless in his bed for another quarter-hour. He very quietly opened his eyes. All the shadows were in the right places. He experimented with stopping his raspy breathing; nothing in the vast chamber moved.

Then very quickly he threw off the bedclothes, bound on his sandals, and slipped out the window into the moonlight.

CHAPTER 5

THE FOREST OF ARCHES

IT WAS about six feet down from the window to the promenade of the Great Colonnade, but the Emperor had discovered the trick of letting himself dangle from the sill gradually until his feet touched the ground. Climbing back up would be a bit more of a chore, but he had learned to manage that too.

And now he was outside, and unsupervised: it was the most delicious thrill of his life, though he knew that, as always, he would pay for it in guilt later on, and would have to make a confession to the Archeparch. But that was later: right now he was outside, and the moon was bright, and he had several hours to spend in his own private world—assuming he could get there without alerting some well-intentioned guard on night watch.

Silently he slipped from the promenade into one of the passages into the residential section; then left and almost immediately right, and then into the Aviary.

It was one of the many marvels of the palace: a vast structure, even longer than the Hall of Lions, with so many windows and skylights that it seemed as though heaven itself was the ceiling. Exotic birds from all over the world flew free in it during the day; but all was silence at night, and the moonlight turned all the rare tropical trees to silver. Slowly and warily the Emperor padded down the serpentine brick walkway that led from one end to the other, keeping an eye on the path in front of him to make sure no noisy bird had bedded down for the night there.

He had almost made it to the end when there was suddenly a loud, sharp voice in his ear:

"Supersubstantial bread!"

The Emperor nearly jumped out of his robes. But it was only Alexius the crow.

"Supersubstantial bread! Where's my supersubstantial bread?"

Alexius had a considerable repertory of things he could say, and the Master of the Birds had tried very hard to teach him to say "Greetings, your clemency," whenever the Emperor came near. But the Archeparch one day had taught Alexius to say "Where's my supersubstantial bread?"—and ever after that it was the thing Alexius was most likely to say, because it earned him a piece of bread most of the time.

"Quiet, Alexius," the Emperor whispered.

"Supersubstantial bread!" the crow called out. "Where's my supersubstantial bread?"

"I didn't bring any bread," the Emperor whispered. He should have remembered the bread. He moved on, but behind him Alexius was still saying "Supersubstantial bread!"

Silently passing through the two sets of doors at the

end of the Aviary, and hoping that no one would think anything of Alexius' outburst, the Emperor turned left and walked out into the open air of the Arcade, a roofed sloping walkway with broad steps that led up the hill behind the Aviary. And at the top he reached his destination. The world knew nothing about it, and it was his own. It was the Forest of Arches by moonlight.

Once, uncounted centuries ago, great kings had ruled from this spot: men whose deeds were recorded in epics so ancient that the archaic language of them required a special study to understand. They had built their palace higher up from the shore, and they had added to it over the many generations of their kingdom. And then they had vanished, and the palace sat vacant; and when, centuries later, the Empire had established its capital here on the spot that guarded the meeting of the seas, the ancient ruins had been too beautiful to destroy. So the bewildering labyrinth of roofless halls and chambers had been turned into the Emperor's private pleasure garden, and the current Emperor was often taken there with a large retinue in fine weather to enjoy a picnic among the artistically landscaped ruins.

But that was in the daylight. No one came to the Forest of Arches at night, because of the ghosts.

A gentle warm breeze was blowing from the sea, picking up the scents of roses and mignonette as it came inland, and then getting lost in the ruins, whirling and eddying, stirring up a few dry leaves in a corner, making a scrubby tree that grew on top of a broken gateway dance against the moon. The breeze whispered, but there were other sounds as well: the sea in the distance, an owl somewhere, a skittering that might have been some small animal or just a dry leaf blowing along the ground. Above all there was the song the moonbeams sang, a high, pure piping that could only be heard in the mind: to the Emperor it always seemed like something between a soft flute and distant bells. The melody was in the patterns of moonbeams and shadows: four long streaks of moonlight pouring between the columns of a ruined portico made a chord; a broad pool of moonlight on the remnants of a mosaic floor was a heavy bass note; the shadow of a vine blowing in the breeze was a trill. No one else knew about the music of the moonlight—no one but the Emperor and the ghosts.

Everyone knew there were ghosts in the Forest of Arches at night. The Emperor didn't doubt it in the least. He had probably seen some of them. The moonlight and shadows played odd tricks on the eyes, but still there were some things that could hardly be anything but ghosts: the soft footsteps that ceased when he looked in their direction, the little round figure he had seen dashing between the shadows on two or three occasions. How could ruins so ancient escape being haunted by their former residents?

But the Emperor was not afraid of the ghosts. On the contrary, he was grateful to them. They were the reason everyone else stayed out of the Forest of Arches by moonlight. The ghosts were his friends: they had never done him any harm, and they gave him the gift of a private world that no one else could enter.

He strolled slowly across the roofless basilica that must have been the ancient kings' audience-hall. There was a destination to be reached, but it would be a terrible waste to get there too quickly. This world was his own in a way that the Empire was not: in fact the Empire owned the Emperor. But the Emperor owned the Forest of Arches in the moonlight by right of conquest. He imagined the great kings of the heroic era receiving their vassals in the great hall, and then walking through the maze of passages prepared to do heroic things whenever the occasion called for them. Exactly what heroic things the ancient heroes did hardly mattered: they were heroic by nature, and even when they were just walking from dinner to the bath, they would have walked heroically. Walking in their footsteps, doing what no one else dared do, the Emperor could be a hero, too.

No one really knew the purposes of all the ancient halls and chambers and passages. Clearly the ancients had built them over a long period, in many different styles; and if there had been any overall plan by which the complex grew, no one now could discern it. Scholars disagreed, since it is the business of scholars to disagree. It was usually said that, like the later and much larger imperial palace that surrounded it, the palace of the ancient kings had simply grown haphazardly, with each new king contributing his own structures and follies as the fancy struck him. But some antiquarians insisted that the complexity of the design could not have arisen by chance. The whole Forest of Arches, they said, was a deliberate labyrinth, designed to confuse and overwhelm any invader. Certainly it was easy to get lost if you didn't know the way. But the Emperor did know the way.

Across the basilica, down the broad passage whose walls (where they still stood) bore eroded reliefs of ancient battles, into a kind of atrium or courtyard; turn right down a row of columns that now held up nothing but the starry sky, left into the first of a series of interconnecting chambers whose vaulted roofs now lay on the ground as piles of stone and brick overgrown with morning glories (the Master of the Gardens was very fond of morning glories), and at last the destination: a small chamber, its roof still partly in place, with a great rectangular stone table at the far end. The moonlight came in through the open part of the roof to illuminate the whole chamber, and the remainder of the roof gave the place a sense of shelter. The antiquarians said that this had been the inner chamber of a temple of one of the barbaric heathen cults to which the ancient heroes were regrettably addicted, and the great stone block or table had been the altar on which bloody sacrifices were offered to the cruel demons the ancients worshiped as gods.

But for the Emperor the place had a different meaning altogether. It was small and sheltered. He sat on the old altar and let his imagination fill in a picture for him. It was a picture of a young man who was not an Emperor at all, who was not even anybody important; but he had a little house, and he lived in his little house, and no one cared what he did there, and no one bothered him at all, and he was happy.

CHAPTER 6

THE CHURCH OF THE ASSUMPTION

"IMPURE thoughts," said the Archeparch, "are of course sinful to some degree, but an Emperor is not held to the same standard of purity as a common tradesman. It has long been accepted that, by taking upon himself the burden of governing his vast realm, the Emperor has earned for himself the right to a certain amount of indulgence in the pleasures of the flesh."

"The problem is that a common tradesman has the right, in all purity, to a wife who loves him," the Emperor replied. "I can't have that, because I have to marry a girl I've never met, and I have to wait nine years to do it."

"There are other expedients."

"Well, yes, for, you know, *that*, but not for love. Nobody *loves* me."

"Love," the Archeparch said very seriously, "is for ordinary commoners. For an Emperor there is reverence, not love."

The Emperor sighed. Why did wealth and power and honor have to make a man so miserable?—But it was time to confess the real sin. He had thought he might get by with impure thoughts, but the Archeparch would hardly even deign to count those as sinful. He had no sense of having lightened his burden. The weight of guilt was still on his shoulders.

"I slipped out into the Forest of Arches again last night," he said very quietly.

The Archeparch was silent for a few moments, and then spoke in a lower voice: "That is a more serious matter."

"I know it's wrong to be deceptive. But those are the only times I can be by myself. Any ordinary man can be by himself whenever he likes, but the Emperor—"

"The Emperor, your clemency, is not an ordinary man. He has a responsibility far beyond the ordinary. If you were to lose your way there in that labyrinth—"

"I'd never lose my way. I know every chamber and passage."

"But there are spirits that haunt the place, or so it is said. Suppose—"

"Oh, the ghosts never bother me. They mind their own business."

"The main thing is," said the Archeparch, "that it is wrong to deceive, especially when the men you are deceiving are men who have nothing but your welfare in mind. They have sworn to protect you, because it is absolutely essential that the Empire continue, and for that there must be an Emperor. You have not yet produced an heir—"

"Well, that's not my fault. I didn't negotiate the treaty with the Sultan. I mean, it was very nice of him to beget a daughter just for me, but I would have accepted one of the ones he already had. I could have started right away and had an heir ready by now."

"You seem to be a little impatient," said the Archeparch.

The Emperor sighed again. He *was* impatient, perhaps; but he was impatient with the whole business of being the living embodiment of empire. At last he asked, "So what should I do?"

The Archeparch thought for a moment and then suggested, "Have you considered calling for a harlot? I can recommend a very discreet service."

"I meant for my penance."

"Oh, that—well, I think three Our Fathers should do it. You can say them while I'm getting ready for the liturgy and get it out of the way."

"Is that all?" the Emperor asked. "Wasn't it a serious sin?"

"In an Emperor," the Archeparch declared gravely, "no sin can really be regarded as serious."

The Emperor thought about those words as he waited in the narthex of the Church of the Assumption and quietly said his three Our Fathers. A common tradesman could sin huge sins. Even a Senator could sin in a large way if he put his mind to it. But an Emperor couldn't even do that. The privilege of sinning was denied to him —and thus the privilege of repentance as well. He felt as though he could be really human if he could repent of something, truly and sincerely, and then know that it was forgiven and everything was all right. But that apparently didn't happen to Emperors. If an Emperor couldn't really sin, then an Emperor was unforgivable.

But then it was time to begin the procession, and the Emperor could forget his moderately gloomy thoughts as

he walked with slow dignity into the nave. The slow dignity came naturally to him here. A cantor filled the vast
space with an ancient chant in proper liturgical language,
not the debased dialect of the present day. (There was a
cantor because the Archeparch had a voice a bit like a
donkey with a head cold.) Above the windows on either
side was a parade of saints, men and women of the distant
past whose exceptional piety had earned them an immortal portrait in mosaic, not to mention a place in heaven. It
must have been much easier to be a saint when one was
not an Emperor; only one Emperor was represented,
standing at the head of the procession on the right. The
current Emperor always gave a short nod to his sanctified
predecessor when he reached that point and saw St.
Adrianus the Good gazing down on him with intense
tranquility—Adrianus the Good, who was quite a different character from Adrianus the Great (as the Emperor
occasionally observed to himself), who had lived two centuries before the Good and had enlarged the empire to its
greatest extent.

Then there was the marvelous dome that seemed to
float above the center of the church, so many were the
windows around its base; and above him inside the dome,
the Emperor knew, was the great mosaic of the Assumption, which he could not look at right now because it
would not do (as he had been told more than once) for the
Emperor to gawk up at the dome like some bumpkin from
Lesser Occidens who had never seen a dome before. This
was the point at which he turned left, bowing his imperial
head slightly toward the altar as he did so, and made his
way to the imperial throne in the north transept. There
he sat and relaxed a little, while the Consul and the Tri-

bune took their places standing at his right and left, and various other Masters and courtiers took their places behind the throne.

Here the Emperor was happy. Now that he was out of view of the main body of the congregation, he could even look up into the dome if he liked and get at least a sideways view of the Assumption, along with seven of the thirteen Apostles who filled the rest of the dome—the Twelve and Paul, who, however, was not visible to him, being one of the images on the near side of the dome. And here for two hours the Emperor could sit unmolested and hear the heavenly chanting, and see the light from the dome streaming down on the innumerable images of saints, and wait for that indescribably thrilling moment when he walked to the altar and knelt—actually knelt, as if an Emperor might not be the very most important thing in the cosmos—to receive the holy sacrament.

But soon after that the liturgy was over, and the people —all of them employed by the palace in some capacity— poured out through the great western doors and formed two irregular clots on the steps that led down from the great church into the Fountain Court, leaving an open space in the middle for the Emperor and his party to come down the steps between them.

The Consul and the Tribune were not among the party; they had stayed in the church to discuss a few matters of no great importance with the Archeparch. They would be along presently. Meanwhile the Emperor walked out into the sunlight as the man who opened the door, a little round man with slick black hair and an immense black mustache, bowed low. The Emperor continued down the steps, being careful not to trip on his robes, to the Fountain Court, where the water spraying from jars held by nymphs in various unlikely poses cooled the air and filled his ears with pleasant sound. Having performed their function, the crowd of Senators and commoners dispersed and left the Emperor in the company of a few courtiers, who engaged in the sort of elaborately meaningless conversation that courtiers make when the focus of the court is present.

The Consul and the Tribune, meanwhile, were having a more meaningful conversation with the Archeparch. They were wearing their serious faces to let the Archeparch know that it was a serious subject.

"We are worried," the Consul told the Archeparch.

"Very worried," the Tribune added, so that he would have something to add to the conversation.

"The Emperor is," the Consul continued;—and then he paused and searched for a word. He began again: "The Emperor is becoming difficult to manage. We were wondering whether there was anything you could tell us."

"I did suggest a harlot," the Archeparch said.

"What I mean," the Consul continued, "is this: you are the Emperor's confessor."

"That is true," the Archeparch agreed.

The Consul looked at the Tribune, and the Tribune at the Consul. The Archeparch was not making this easy.

"He means," said the Tribune, "that we were wondering, you might say, if, or rather whether, you might tell us whether he happened to mention anything that might be in some way useful to know."

"Now, you know I can never speak of what I've heard in confession," the Archeparch replied.

"But under the circumstances," said the Consul, "would you not have a positive duty to the Empire—"

"I have told you, I can never *speak* of what I've heard in confession," the Archeparch repeated with a very significant emphasis.

The Consul looked down and saw that the Archeparch was making some very obvious gestures.

The Consul sighed, and only long practice in courtly politeness prevented him from rolling his eyes. He hated to do it this way, but if it was the only way around the Archeparch's conscience...

"Two syllables," the Consul said, watching the Archeparch's hands very carefully. "First syllable... Sounds like..."

CHAPTER 7

THE WAR IN THE EAST

IT TOOK two firm thwacks from the Master of the Beasts to make the lion roar the next morning. It was quite a relief for everyone when it did: time had frozen for a while as everyone stood still, staring at the floor—everyone but the Emperor, who had a fine view of the tops of everyone's heads, but much preferred seeing their faces. When at last the lion had roared, he could go on with the audience and get it out of the way.

"The Emperor's compliments to the Senate and People," he said as the lion creaked back into its resting position,

The Consul replied, "The greetings of the Senate to the Emperor, the bearer of their burdens."

The Tribune replied, "The greetings of the People to the Emperor, the guardian of their rights."

"And now," said the Emperor, "what is the business of the day?"

"First," said the Consul, "there is the matter of the gift for the Sultan's collection."

"How's that coming along?"

The Tribune spoke: "With your clemency's kind indulgence, the guild of weavers has submitted a very fine tapestry."

"Already? Goodness."

"We have assigned the Master of the Treasury the task of keeping the entries safely until your clemency can judge them," the Consul explained as a preface to shouting, "The Master of the Treasury!"

"The Master of the Treasury!" the tenth guard on the right called out.

"The Master of the Treasury!" the twentieth guard on the left called out.

"The Master of the Treasury!" the thirtieth guard on the right called out.

The grey-headed man entered and began the long march from the back of the hall. Without the huge pile of jewels in front of him, he was a rather more impressive figure: he walked with a comfortable dignity that made him look taller than he was. Behind him came a pair of strong men carrying something that looked like an enormous scroll; they marched with as much dignity as was possible for two men carrying an enormous scroll, but the thing was awkward, and the Emperor had the impression that, but for his august presence, the men would be cursing right now.

It took some time for the little procession to reach the mosaic of Adrianus XVII, during which all the Emperor could do was sit and look imperial to the best of his ability, in spite of a strong desire to reach around and scratch just below the shoulder blades, where the imperial robe somehow managed to be itchiest. He wondered whether it would be possible to set the thing on fire by some sort of unfortunate accident, and then escape from the robe soon enough to avoid being singed but, alas, too late to save the robe itself. Probably not.

When at last the three men stopped in front of the imperial dais, the Master of the Treasury bowed, and the two men set the great scroll up on its two posts and laboriously unrolled it.

Marvelous things began to appear. It was a tapestry with a background of deep indigo, on which, in the foreground, dozens of ships appeared in artistic confusion; and, as more of it was revealed, the Emperor could see that behind them was the Palace itself, as seen from the sea somewhere near the entrance to the Gulf of the Heptapolis. There was the Pharos by the Inlet; above and behind it the Terrace Garden, and the dome of the Church of the Assumption; and high on the Eminence stood the Tower of Diotrephes, And now that more ships were visible it was clear that this was a great naval battle, with soldiers boarding a ship here and falling into the water there, and ships on fire, and oars stirring the sea to a froth. The two men with the poles finished unrolling the tapestry and stood at either end, leaning away from their poles to stretch the picture flat.

"It's magnificent," the Emperor declared. He rose from his throne and stepped down to take a closer look, "And the Guild of Weavers produced this in two days?" He pointed at it with the sword of Adrianus XXI.

The Tribune glanced up at the Consul, and then carefully explained, "It is my *understanding*, your clemency, that the Guild, anticipating that a work of this sort night, on some occasion, be demanded, had, in fact, begun, on their own initiative, which is very laudable, some time ago."

Which meant, as the Emperor knew, that the whole contest of the guilds had been worked out months earlier, and had really been presented to him for his approval only when most of the work had already been done. It was the way most things were accomplished: the Emperor had absolute power in theory, but in practice was spared the labor of exercising it.

"It's the Battle of the Gulf, isn't it?" said the Emperor, taking a close look at a remarkably well-rendered galley ramming another, with oars sticking out in all directions in the moment of panic,

"Yes, your clemency," said the Tribune.

"A very appropriate subject," the Consul added, "It was the first battle in which the Sultan's navy fought alongside ours, thus—"

"—thus establishing the friendly relations that have persisted to this day," the Emperor continued, "with a long line of Sultans who have been loyal vassals of the Emperors. And what a glorious victory! The Aspersian fleet had half again as many ships as our alliance, but Adrianus XIX waited till they were bottled up in the entrance to the Gulf and then drove a wedge of galleys right into their fleet. Look—here's Number Nineteen himself leaping from his sinking flagship to capture the Aspersian galley!"

"A thrilling moment, your clemency," the Consul remarked.

"It certainly was. Thrilling moments like that never happen to me. Number Nineteen saved the seven cities, His example probably inspired the victory. I never get to inspire anybody."

"Your ancestors earned for you the blessing of a strong

Empire," said the Consul. "That is why the Aspersian border is now a great distance away. The Aspersian war need never inconvenience you,"

"It's going well, then?"

"Oh, very well," the Tribune said, "Devastating victories. Our generals keep smashing the Aspersian army to atoms."

"And yet it never stays smashed," the Emperor said.

"Well," said the Tribune, but nothing more seemed to be ready to come out of his mouth.

"There are a great many Aspersians," the Consul explained helpfully. "That is why the Aspersian war has continued for centuries. There is always an Aspersian war, and there will always be an Aspersian war. It is part of the marvelous order of the cosmos."

"But don't you think we could do better than that?" the Emperor asked. "Eudoxia the Great led her army personally, and they won such a resounding victory that the Aspersians didn't recover for a generation. And Adrianus XIX—he leaped on that Aspersian galley just as his own was going under"—the Emperor turned and leaped to the first step of the imperial dais—"and slash!"—he slashed the air in front of him with the sword of Adrianus XXI—"the captain was gone! And then without even looking behind him, slash!"—the Emperor slashed behind him—

There was a noise, or rather a series of noises: they sounded like *Rip, thud-thud, clack clack clackclackack-ackack.*

The Emperor didn't really want to turn and look, but he did anyway.

The two strong men were quickly picking themselves

up off the floor. Their poles lay beside them, each with half a tapestry still attached; it had been divided near the middle by what had started as a neat diagonal cut but grew more ragged toward the bottom.

"I—," the Emperor began, and then he decided to begin again, "Doubtless a little careful stitching will..."

"Let it be noted," said the admirably unruffled Consul, "that the Emperor has judged the entry of the Weavers and found it insufficiently rare and exquisite."

"I was just... a little carried away, you see. I mean, I was imagining how having their Emperor lead them personally would make quite an impression on the troops." He looked at the Consul with a frightened-puppy smile. "Wouldn't it?"

"Possibly a fatal one, your clemency," said the Consul.

"I wouldn't have to have the sword," the Emperor said quietly.

"The Emperor's place is at the heart of the Empire," the Consul explained with one of his very patient smiles. "From here the warmth of his radiance flows and vivifies the whole body of the state, from the western reaches of Greater Occidens to the Aspersian border. Move the heart, and the body will no longer function; put it in the east, and the West will suffer and wither."

"Or you might say you're like the stomach," the Tribune suggested. Feeling the oppressive wall of silence that followed his remark, he looked up at the Consul's carefully composed face and added, "I mean, because he's right in the center... of the.... body...."

Without detectably moving a single facial muscle, the Consul somehow managed to freeze the Tribune with his eyes.

The Emperor ascended the dais and sat back down on his throne. "Of course," he said, "I understand: it's always best for me to be where I've always been and do what I've always done."

"Precisely," the Consul agreed with an expression of profound relief. "That is how the Empire works."

CHAPTER 8

THE MONAD AND THE DYAD

THE EMPEROR was paying very close attention to his philosophy lesson, because it kept him from going back to the tapestry and wondering whether he might not have made such a fool of himself if this or that had happened differently—if, for example, he had taken his philosophy lesson before the audience, as he often did, or if...

But it was best just to pay close attention to Iamblichus, who was forming a circle with both hands and must therefore be about to demonstrate something important.

"By the contemplation of itself, the monad gives birth"—Iamblichus moved his hands apart and made a circle with each one—"to the dyad."

"How does that work?" the Emperor asked, forcing himself to take a keen interest in the monad and the dyad.

"You see, the monad is both the subject and the object of its own contemplation. Unity becomes multiplicity,"

"So if I think about myself long enough, there will be two of me?"

Iamblichus sighed, and then, halfway through the

sigh, remembered to suppress it. "No. It doesn't work that way."

"Why not? I am contemplating, and I am contemplating myself. Subject and object."

"It only works for the monad, That is how the monad becomes the dyad, but it—"

"Well, then, when did the monad start to contemplate itself?"

Iamblichus explained it patiently, though he appeared to think it ought to be obvious, "The monad always contemplates itself. That is its nature."

"Then it seems to me that there never was a monad. There was always a dyad."

For just a moment, a strange expression flitted across the philosopher's face—an expression that might have been rage, or might have been despair. But by the time he spoke, it had been replaced by a bland smile. "Isn't it time for your dancing lesson?" he asked.

"History," said the Emperor. "Today, history is next."

"Then it is time for Philosophy to make way for History." And with a few more words—because Iamblichus always had a few more words—he took his leave and was gone.

The Emperor stood and gazed across the Narrows for a while. It seemed to him that he must always be a monad who would never give birth to a dyad. Surrounded by courtiers and guards and tutors, he was all alone, with no one who could—

And all at once the Emperor realized that, in fact, he was alone, not just metaphorically but physically. Iamblichus the philosophy tutor had left before Sozomen the history tutor had arrived. An irresistible urge came over the Emperor: before he had even made a conscious decision, he and walked down the steps from the Stoa and was strolling along the shore of the Narrows, looking sometimes across the water to the great city over there, sometimes ahead of him to the fine houses and sub-palaces of the senatorial quarter, until a strong scent of anise attracted his attention, and he saw that he had come to the corner of the kitchen garden that reached down to the Narrows, and there was anise hyssop bloom-ing there; and the low hum of the bees on the flowers, mixed with the sounds of the lapping waves and the calls of the gulls, made a stroll in the garden seem very attrac-tive. And why not? He bent down and picked a leaf of the anise hyssop, and he sniffed at it as he stepped into the garden.

This was a garden he never got to see. When he was given an afternoon out in a garden, it was always in the Terrace Garden or the Forest of Arches, which were beautiful places; but they were pleasure gardens, and this was a working garden, which made it more of a pleasure to him. These plants had jobs to do: every one of them went into food, and was therefore food itself. As he looked up the slope, he saw wonderful plots of herbs—chamomile, mints of all sorts, dill or fennel or something. And then above them was the orchard, where he could wander and pick a peach right off the tree, and literally eat the fruit of his own labor, which would be an utterly novel experience——

"If your clemency is ready now," said the Consul, "Sozomen is waiting for your history lesson."

They were both there, right behind him—the Consul

and the Tribune. How had they found him almost instantly? Once again, he felt the weight of guilt descending on him, when just moments before he had been filled with a sense of joyous possibility.

They didn't even scold him on the way back to the Stoa. They just acted as if of course he had been waiting for them to show up so that he could get on with his history lesson. It would have been infuriating, except that the feeling of guilt left no room in the Emperor's heart for anger at the moment.

And so in a few minutes he was back on the Stoa, where Sozomen was busy leading him through his current favorite project, which was dividing all the Emperors of history into Good and Wicked. History, Sozomen believed, was fundamentally a branch of ethics, and its purpose was to provide useful examples of virtue and vice to illustrate the conclusions of moral philosophy.

"So—Eudoxia the Great," Sozomen asked: "Good or Wicked?"

"Well, Good, obviously," the Emperor replied.

"No, your clemency. Eudoxia was a Wicked Empress."

"Why? She rooted out the usurper who killed her husband Adrianus XIV. She led her army to a victory that crippled Aspersia for a generation. She stamped out corruption in the provinces and made the first peace treaty with the Sultan. She was a famous patron of the arts, and under her the Empire reached its greatest extent in three centuries, We even call her 'the Great,' don't we?"

"But she was a woman," Sozomen explained.

"My mother was a woman, I presume. Wasn't she? And I never heard anyone call her wicked."

"Certainly not, clemency. But she did not aspire to the imperial throne. It is Wicked for a woman to take the place of a man."

"Why?"

"It is in the nature of things for women to be subservient to men. It is Wicked to defy nature."

"So it would have been better for her to leave the Empire to rot under that cretin Licinius?"

"No, not as such," Sozomen said. "Not better. But it is still Wicked for a woman to take the imperial throne.

"So what you're saying is that it doesn't matter what I do, but only what I am—that's what makes something moral or immoral?"

Sozomen smiled the smile of a man who would prefer to be somewhere else. "That would be," he said hesitantly, "a good question to take up with our friend Iamblichus."

And below in the shadows, where they listened very intently to every word, the Consul and the Tribune looked at each other, and the Tribune shrugged.

Some time later, after the Emperor had been taken to prepare for his salt-water bathing expedition, the Consul and the Tribune had a brief opportunity for a private discussion, and the Tribune was able to articulate some of his worries.

"We could have lost him," he said, "The Su—— Our patron would not be pleased if he wandered out on his own."

"And went where?" the Consul asked rhetorically. "There is only one exit through the Wall, and the guards have very simple and explicit instructions. Do you expect him to swim? He has never been taught to swim—we

made sure of that. No, I think we can trust the arrangements we've made for his...for his safety. His nocturnal
excursions have been harmless."

"I still think we ought to be more careful."

"And I think," said the Consul, "that we can afford to
let our Emperor enjoy a little privacy sometimes. Just as
long as there's somebody watching him all the time."

Meanwhile the Emperor had been changed into his
bathing robes, which were much like his ordinary day
robes, except that it would never do for him to go on a
bathing expedition in his ordinary day robes, Alone, with
no one but the usual small army of silent valets and servants, he was once again tormented by private thoughts.
It was stupid and wrong to have been so careless with the
Sword of Adrianus XXI. And when he had wandered off
into the kitchen garden, had he not betrayed the trust of
his most loyal ministers? Yet no one would ever accuse
him of having done anything wrong.

What if he had been a bit more careless with the
sword? Probably the result would have been no different.
Probably if he had accidentally bisected the Tribune instead of the tapestry, the Consul would simply have declared that the Emperor had executed the Tribune for
certain good and sufficient reasons. As Emperor he could
do no real wrong—and yet the Emperor was somehow
made to feel as if everything he did was wrong, if it was
done without the approval of the Consul and the Tribune,
But he could never be sorry for it if no one admitted it
was wrong. He felt as though he had rolled in wrongness
and could never get the stench of it off.

And there was no one to listen to him sympathetically.
Even the Archeparch refused to call him a sinner. The

Emperor, as Emperor, was a monad who could never manage to become a dyad. Would Spring Blossom Et Cetera change him? Would they be a dyad together? Could he really wait nine years to find out?

And then he was dressed, and the Consul and the Tribune were there, and it was time to see whether a saltwater bath would wash away any of the wrongness that clung to him.

CHAPTER 9

THE POOL OF ST. TRYPHAENA

THE INLET is a narrow arm reaching into the palace grounds from the Gulf of the Heptapolis; it is probably natural, though so many generations of kings and Emperors have made practical and whimsical improvements to the coastline that it might well have been dug in ancient times for unknowable reasons. And if the Inlet is an arm, then the Pool of St. Tryphaena is its fist, an artificially enlarged saltwater basin, roughly oval in shape, that is the focus of a broad pleasure ground. On the southern shore is the theater, from which the audience looks across the stage to the pool itself, and behind it the Terrace Garden; and above and behind that to the northwest, the steep forested hills of the Wilderness. On the northeast side, a running brook, more artistically natural than nature could possibly have made it, gurgles and splatters down through the Terrace Garden to end with a musical cascade into the Pool; it originates from the nymphs in the Fountain Court, whose forms can just occasionally be glimpsed through the leaves of the Terrace Garden. And as the eye continues to ascend, it will see some of the tops of the fine buildings that surround the

Fountain, and further up the ruins that make up the Forest of Arches, and then, standing over everything else with inescapable authority, the almost frightfully tall Tower of Diotrephes, with its tragic associations. Considering the fine view from every seat, the only possible complaint a theatergoer could have is that no tragedy could equal the grandeur, no comedy the diverting amusement, of such a backdrop.

Of course the Emperor knew he would not have much time to enjoy the view. He had not come for the view. He had come because his physician believed that a saltwater bath was a cure for just about anything, and a fine preventative when nothing in particular was wrong, and had directed that the Emperor be given one at least twice a week. And of course it was not at all possible for an Emperor just to take off his robes and swim, much as he might like to do so. First of all, he had never been taught to swim; second, the bath had to be accomplished while maintaining the imperial dignity, which could not be maintained if anyone happened to see the Emperor undressed who was not specifically authorized to see the Emperor undressed.

"Do you think we could do without the box today?" the Emperor asked quietly, as he often did when he came here. But, as they often did, his ministers pretended not to have heard him.

"The Emperor's bathing-machine!" the Consul called out, and at once there was the ponderous grinding sound of large wheels on stone, and the creaking and groaning of a wooden structure in motion. From behind its artful screen of dense shrubbery came a great wooden cube, painted all over in imperial purple, with carved relief work picked out in gilding all around the cornice. It rolled slowly down a stone trackway toward the water, its progress retarded by four men holding elaborate bronze handles, one at each corner, and trying their best to appear not to be straining.

"I don't think we really need the box," the Emperor said, but to himself, since long experience had taught him that no one else would listen to his objections about the bathing-machine. It continued to roll into the water, and there it stopped, with only the back end still out of the water. Two of the men opened the pair of doors in the rear, and it was time for the Emperor to step inside.

He risked one direct and unignorable appeal to the Consul: "Do you think it would be possible this time for me to bathe outside the box?"

"The imperial dignity, your clemency," the Consul replied. It was a subject that needed no predicate.

The Emperor stood patiently while someone removed his sandals. Meanwhile soft carpets were laid along the short distance between the Emperor and the bathing-machine; and once the sandals were gone the Emperor padded his way over to the door, took a last look at the beauty around him, and stepped into the darkness. The doors closed behind him.

It was not utterly dark, of course. A few sheepish and apologetic rays of light sidled in through slits near the roof of the box, cleverly hidden among the carved details from outside observers. Once his eyes adjusted to the sudden leap from bright sunlight to dim interior, the Emperor could see quite well. He sat on the bench with its luxurious cushions and waited, and in a few moments there was a very slight jolt, and the thing was moving

again, rolling down into the water, until the water inside
the box was almost knee-deep. This was as far as it would
go. It had occurred to him more than once that anyone
who wanted to assassinate an Emperor had only to keep
pushing the box until the water was up to the roof; but
that never happened, because in all his life there had
never been anyone who wanted to assassinate the Emperor. In past ages Emperors had worried about such
things, but not in his time. In the current day nothing bad
ever happened, because nothing ever happened at all.

Now it was time to wash—as if it would really clean
him to wash in the Pool of St. Tryphaena. This was the
water that washed the body but left the soul quite macu-
late. He got the robes off and hung them on the gilt
bronze hook that hung from the ceiling, and then gradually lowered himself into the cool water. He thought
briefly, as he had thought before more than once, that
there was enough space under the walls of the box for
him to slip out and swim away, but that thought presup-
posed that he knew how to swim, which he didn't, and
that there was somewhere to go. He could be a hermit
somewhere in the Wilderness: that would be a pleasant
life, but he would like to have some clothes to start with,
and he would like not to drown before he got there. So,
as he imagined escaping from his routine, he picked up
the pumice stone and the soap ball, and followed his routine. And when he was finished, he imagined how amusing it would be to see the faces of his ministers if he left
his imperial bathing robes and just walked out naked; but
of course he didn't, because it wasn't the sort of thing an
Emperor did. He dried himself off, put on his robes, sat
on the bench, pulled the silken cord that rang the little

bell, and rode the machine back up out of the water.

And then the Emperor went back, just as he always did; and he was dressed in his dinner robes, which were hard to distinguish from his bathing robes, but it would never do for him to go to dinner in anything other than his dinner robes. And then he had dinner, as he always did; and he read an improving book, as he always did (how he longed for the days of his youth, when the books had had stories in them); and he went to bed, as he always did; and he fooled the musicians, as he always did.

He had thought for a while that he might have to forgo his night out in the Forest of Arches. This was the last night the moon would be bright enough (he had very strict standards for lunar brightness), but earlier in the evening the clouds had obscured the moon, and it had seemed as if he would have to wait another three weeks. But then the clouds parted, and the waning gibbous moon shone bright and yellow, and the Emperor slipped out the window.

This time he had remembered to bring a few bread-crumbs for Alexius, who only had to ask him once to receive his daily bread. The drifting remnants of clouds gave the sky texture, complementing the ragged ruins in the Forest of Arches; and when he reached the little chamber and sat on the altar, the Emperor spent quite some time looking up at the moon.

It seemed to him that he and the moon had quite a bit in common. The moon was also unique: it was a monad that would never be a dyad. It grew over time, and then diminished, and eventually vanished entirely, only to run through the whole cycle again—just as an Emperor began small, and grew great, and then aged and faded, until at last he was replaced by a new Emperor, who must run through the same course. He wondered whether he was a waxing Emperor, or whether he had already begun to wane, and how long it would be until his light failed utterly. The clouds danced across the face of the moon, but the moon could never join their dance; just as the Emperor was the immovable center on which the whole Empire turned, but he himself never partook in any of the activity. He watched the clouds roll across the face of the moon, some of them transparent, some thick and opaque; and so lost was he in his meditations that the Emperor did not notice until the edge of the bank was already very near the moon that the smaller clouds were the vanguard of a large bank of clouds moving in from the west.

That was not good. The Emperor leaped up and walked as fast as he dared, but he had only made it as far as the row of columns before the moon was devoured by the advancing cloud, and the pale light failed and was extinguished, and he was left in darkness that pressed like a blanket against his eyes.

He knew his way around the Forest of Arches better than anyone but the Master of the Gardens, he told himself. There were six more columns until he came to the atrium. Or was it five? Almost certainly six. A very strong probability of six.

He would have to go on: he would have to be in bed before dawn. If it was discovered that he had left his bed —Well, the Emperor could do no wrong, so there would be no real consequences, except for the worst consequence he could possibly imagine, which was that he would be prevented from slipping out into the Forest of Arches by moonlight ever again.

Reaching out with his left hand, he felt one of the columns, right where it ought to have been. And the border of sweet alyssum was tickling his toes through the sandals. If he followed that border, he should be safe from missteps until the border ended, and that would be the entrance to the atrium. And then—but it was better to solve one problem at a time. He walked slowly forward. dragging his toes lightly through the alyssum. There were still stars in part of the sky, and some of the ruins outlined themselves against the spangled field, giving him a sense of where he was. But the cloud bank was rapidly eating up the stars as well. He moved as quickly as he could move while dragging his left foot through the alyssum, but by the time the Emperor reached what he was almost certain was the atrium, the stars were almost entirely gone.

He shuffled carefully into the atrium and decided that the safe thing would be to follow the perimeter rather than try to navigate the irregularly curved path through the gardens in the center. Slowly he felt his way—a border of thyme helped him here—until he was convinced he had found the gap he wanted, the one that led into the hall of reliefs. And as he felt his way along the long wall, he was sure he had been right; until suddenly there was a wall in front of him that had no right to be there, and he was sure he had been wrong. There was no way to go but right, so he went right. And then there was no way to go but left, so he went left. And soon he knew that he was completely lost.

The stars were all gone now. There was nothing to see. But in the darkness there was quite a bit to hear, and the Emperor began to imagine that he could hear the ghosts

of the ancients. An owl spoke—or was it the spirit of
some long-dead lady repeating her dying sigh forever?
The breeze was picking up; there was a chill in the air;
and the leaves whispered a message from the chorus of
vanished heroes—a message at the edge of intelligibility,
whose syllables in the heroic dialect must have been
telling him what to do, if only he had paid more attention
to his epic grammar.

How could he find his way? The Emperor's residence
was downhill from the Forest of Arches: that should help.
But the ground was very irregular, and although downhill
was a good general principle, it would be hard to apply.
The individual halls and chambers of the ancient ruins
had flat floors, of course; they often connected to the next
chamber by some number of steps, but how to find those
steps—and how to avoid falling down them, though admittedly that would be an efficient way of finding them—
was a question whose answer eluded the Emperor at the
moment. The dispiriting fact was that he was lost in a
dark labyrinth, and without a miracle he would not find
his way out before morning.

And then the miracle came—just when he least expected it, which of course is the proper time for a miracle.

He was still shuffling forward in the darkness, more
and more cautiously as more and more potential catastro-
phes formed in his imagination, when he saw a doorway,
or at least a gap in the wall, ahead and on the right. He
saw it: somewhere there was light, and enough of it was
escaping to make a dim outline of that doorway against
the blackness. Any light at all was a miracle. It gave him
hope just when he had despaired. He shuffled a little

faster until he reached the doorway.

And he could plainly see now where the light was coming from. Across a broad hall—which now he recognized by its shape as the one with the dolphin mosaics, so he knew where he was—he saw a doorway from which light was streaming.

Who was there? It was outside the Forest of Arches, in part of the palace that held the kitchens and pantries and other utilitarian rooms he seldom saw. Of course if he went in there someone might discover him, and it might be reported to the Consul.

But he really had only two choices. He could wander aimlessly in the darkness, or he could walk toward the light.

So he walked toward the light.

CHAPTER 10

PULCHERIA

IT WAS almost blinding in its intensity at first, after the palpable blackness of the labyrinth; but it was only the ordinary light of the ordinary lanterns in the room. It was a pantry or something—some sort of room in which things were stored, to judge by the shelves full of jars and bins that lined the walls. In the middle of it was a woman on her knees, her back to the doorway, a bucket by her side, a brush in her hand. She was scrubbing the mosaic tiles vigorously, and she was faced the other way, so she didn't see the Emperor in the doorway.

If he could just sneak past behind her—

"You'd better have taken your shoes off," the scrubbing woman said without looking up.

"I, well—" He automatically began untying his sandals.

"Everyone thinks these floors just clean themselves," the woman continued. She dipped the brush in the bucket and sloshed it around. "Well, they don't. *I* clean them." She brought the brush out of the bucket and started scrubbing again. "Every night, all night, I scrub the floors, clean as a dinner plate, just in case the Emperor happens to come in and fall on his imperial arse."

"Is that likely?" the Emperor asked. He had his sandals off now and was standing on the cold bare floor. That never happened to him in the normal course of things, and he was enjoying the sensation.

"Ha," said the woman. It was a "ha" that managed to convey a great deal of contempt for Emperors.

"So you think the floor is not likely to make the acquaintance of the imperial arse?" the Emperor asked. He ought to have gone on his way as quickly as he could, but there was something fascinating about this conversation. No one had ever talked to him this way before.

"He doesn't even know this room exists," the woman replied. "He probably thinks food grows on plates. Why would he ever come in here? But I still have to keep it clean for the Emperor. Every night, clean for the Emperor. Clean for the Emperor, every room. It's a good thing I'm a lady, or I'd tell the Emperor what I think."

"I'm sure he'd—"

"I think he ought to get down on his hands and knees for just one day and scrub, that's what I think," she continued to the oddly musical accompaniment of her scrub brush. "I know he's a precious treasure and all that, but I think it would do him some good to do some honest labor for once. It would do me some good to see it, anyway."

There was something wonderfully beautiful about the way the lamplight glinted from her glossy raven hair, and about the way the muscles in her shoulders moved as she scrubbed. The Emperor found himself wanting to keep the conversation going just to enjoy the view. "You think it would help him govern the Empire better?"

She laughed—a sudden burst of music that utterly delighted him. It was her only response, but it was certainly expressive enough.

"You don't think much of the Emperor's government?"

"Well," she said, turning to face him; and it was the last thing she said for quite some time.

She had a beautiful face—not beautiful like a statue of some heathen goddess, but beautiful like the face of a friend, in spite of its current expression of shock and dismay. The purple border had betrayed him: there was no mistaking him for anyone other than the Emperor. But perhaps a friendly word would breach the purple wall.

"You don't have to stop," he said. "I was enjoying hearing what you thought."

She still gaped in mute terror; her dark eyes looked huge in the lamplight, and her lips hung open as if she had lost control of her jaw.

"Really," the Emperor continued, "I'm not at all—"

"I'm going to be boiled in oil," the young woman said.

Now it was the Emperor's turn to express shock. "Boiled in oil?"

"As soon as they can get the cauldron set up."

The Emperor looked down into her eyes and cautiously approached her. "Is it usual for my servants to be deep-fried?"

"It's the punishment for presumption," she said quietly.

"Presumption? There's a crime called 'presumption'? What's 'presumption'?"

Reluctantly, she answered, "For a commoner, talking to the Emperor would do it."

"Really?" He thought for a moment. "But I command

you to talk to me. There—how's that? You can't disobey your Emperor, can you? That would be— It would be *presumption*."

"I—your clemency, you see, we——" She ran out of words.

"I never get to talk to anyone who tells me anything interesting," the Emperor told her. "And by the way, could you stand up? It would be easier to talk to you if you were standing up."

"In the presence of the Emperor—"

"In the presence of the Emperor, shouldn't you do what the Emperor says?" He smiled and held out his hand.

"A commoner can never touch—"

"I'll tell you a secret," said the Emperor, dropping his hand for the moment. "I'm not supposed to be here. If they found out I was out walking in the middle of the night, they'd make sure it never happened again. An Emperor doesn't get to do everything he wants, you know. Sometimes I think an Emperor doesn't get to do *any-thing* he wants. So if you don't tell anyone, my secret is safe. And if my secret is safe, then I was never here, and you never talked to me, and you never touched my hand"—which he now offered her again—"and so I promise you that nothing bad will happen to you if you stand up and talk to me for just a little while."

The woman looked up warily at the extended hand, and then slowly reached out, as if she thought it might burn her, and at last took the Emperor's hand and, with his willing help, pulled herself up.

Now she was standing, looking down at the floor.

"Nothing bad happened to either of us," the Emperor

pointed out.

"Not yet," the woman said quietly.

"I'm not really here," he said in what he hoped was a friendly and encouraging tone. "I'm just— I'm just your perception. You're just imagining the purple border on the robe. You're just imagining that there's such a thing as an Emperor. Really I'm just a man standing on the cold floor in his bare feet—"

"Oh! Oh, your clemency—I'm sorry—put the shoes back on—or—I mean—if you want to—"

"I don't want to. I never get to walk around in bare feet. It's not done. But tonight we're doing things that aren't done. And we're getting away with it! I feel naughty, but I don't care."

The woman laughed. She stopped herself quickly, but she had laughed at him.

"I made you laugh! That's wonderful! Do it again."

And she did. "I'm sorry," she said quickly. "It's just— you're acting like a little boy." She looked up at him with a smile—a real smile, a beautiful smile; not the working smile he usually got from his ministers, a smile that had a job to do and did it and went home, but a smile that just happened.

"Am I?" the Emperor asked. "I wouldn't know, you see. I've never been a little boy."

"Well, of course you have. Even—"

"No, I was never a little boy. I was a small Emperor, and I became a bigger Emperor. But I was never a little boy. I was an orphan, you know, so I had to start early."

"Oh, I'm an orphan, too," the woman said. "I mean— not that it's important..."

"Of course it's important. It's the most important thing

in the world. Right now everything about you is the most important thing in the world. In particular, what's your name?"

"Pulcheria, your clemency."

"Pulcheria! Well, then, Pulcheria, you were telling me what you thought of me, and I didn't want you to stop."

"I didn't really think—"

"You said I should get down on my hands and knees and scrub, didn't you?"

"That was just—I mean, I had no idea I was talking to—"

"It sounded like a good idea."

"Oh, don't— I didn't mean—"

But the Emperor was already on his knees picking up the brush. "Is this how you do it?" He attempted a few strokes with the brush, which caused her to laugh again.

"It would take you days to do this room that way."

"That's not good, I suppose."

"It would put you a little behind in your work. If your clemency will permit—"

She knelt beside him and took the brush.

"Both hands on it, like this, and then I use my weight on it to push it forward, like this. I'm not trying to scrub when I bring it back—that would wear me out. Just pull it back like this, and then I lean on it and scrub forward like this."

He could feel the warmth of her beside him. It was really the first time he could remember having chosen on his own to be close to another human being. The sense of freedom made him feel almost drunk, or at least he imagined this must be what feeling almost drunk was like. He tried a few strokes with the brush; she pronounced his work much improved, which delighted him. "Clean enough for the imperial arse?" he asked her, which made her laugh again.

It would have delighted him to scrub the rest of the night with Pulcheria beside him, but he began to worry again about his absence from the bed he was supposed to be in. "I have to get back before I'm missed and provoke a few stern suggestions from the Consul," he told her. He stood and held out his hand, which this time she took without hesitation as she pulled herself up. "But I'm sure I'll see you again," he continued. "I will, won't I?"

"If you're out wandering in the middle of the night, I scrub all the pantries and the hall in front."

"Then I *will* see you again," he declared. "I'll make it a point. And you can talk to me and not get boiled in oil at all."

Pulcheria was smiling when he left, and she continued smiling for a minute or so after he had gone, until a hood suddenly covered her head, a hand came over her mouth, and strong hands picked her up by arms and feet and carried her away.

CHAPTER 11

AN EXEMPLARY PUNISHMENT

THE Emperor awoke at the prescribed time the next morning and was not tired at all. He had managed to slip out and follow the wall along the Great Colonnade to his window, and then to slip back into bed, and four hours' sleep had been quite enough to refresh him. His first thought was of the night's delightful adventure, and so was his second thought, and his third. He would probably try to get to the pantries again tonight, he decided. But now he had to be dressed in his expedition robes (which were hard to distinguish from his night robes), because, as the imperial valets told him, today he was going on an expedition.

First there was the Emperor's morning tonic to get through, specially prepared by the imperial physician and thus as foul as foul could be; but it was followed by a peach from the orchard in the kitchen garden—the orchard he had been so tantalizingly close to the day before —so the foulness of the tonic was quickly overwhelmed and extinguished. And it was a good day at any rate, and nothing vile could linger long on a good day like this. A few more things were brought for the Emperor to eat, and he did eat a few of them, although as always there seemed to be enough for eight or nine Emperors, and most of it had to be sent away again.

And now it was time for the expedition. An expedition, as he knew, was meant to entertain the Emperor when the Consul and the Tribune had decided that he needed entertaining. He might under other circumstances be inclined to be annoyed by the thought of it; expeditions always offered tantalizing prospects of delights that were, for all sorts of good and proper reasons, denied to Emperors. But the Wilderness was beautiful, and he now had in his own mind a delight of which his ministers knew nothing. He had Pulcheria, the woman whose acquaintance he had chosen to make. No one had chosen for him. He himself had chosen. And she had told him what she actually thought! No one ever did that for him. So he allowed himself to be prepared for the expedition—which meant that he allowed one of the valets to put boots on his feet—and departed with a light heart.

The expedition assembled outside the Hall of Lions in the broad passage that led past the Emperor's own living quarters. The Herald, whose job was to be in front, was in front; then came the Emperor, with the Consul on his right and the Tribune on his left; and behind them was a long line of porters under the direction of the Master of the Porters. Behind them all was the Guide, who would take his place in the front when the party reached the Wilderness, but was not needed in the corridors outside the Emperor's living quarters.

When the expedition had formed a suitably precise line, the long march down the hall began. The Consul, the Tribune, the Herald, the Guide, and the porters with their Master all marched in step; but it was not proper for the Emperor to march in step with them, because the Emperor was above that and must be seen to be above it. Walking with a different stride when everyone else is marching in step is actually rather difficult, and it took a fair amount of concentration to do it. But the Emperor did it, because not doing it would provoke a reminder from the Consul that he ought to be doing it, and nothing was more to be avoided than a reminder from the Consul. So the marching feet echoed down the long, high grand passageway, with the off-rhythm clacking of the Emperor's boots on the mosaic floor as an obbligato.

The Herald reached the end of the passage and made a smart right turn. The Emperor, the Consul, and the Tribune turned behind him, though it was hard to do it smartly when the Emperor was not allowed to walk in step; and the whole procession of porters with baggage followed. This passage was short and led out into the bright sunlight: the clouds of the night before had dropped some rain, scoured the atmosphere clean, and left only a few rapidly drying puddles to remember them by. The walk was now upward toward the Forum, which was some distance up the hill past the Church of the Assumption. But even at this distance it was quite obvious that something was going on up there. A crowd had gathered up on the great open space, and there was quite a lot of noise coming down the hill.

The Herald turned left toward the Terrace Garden, but the Emperor stopped, nearly causing the Consul to collide with him, and actually causing the Master of the Porters to collide with the Consul.

"If your clemency will follow—" the Consul began.

But the Emperor interrupted him:

"What's going on in the Forum?"

"A small matter," the Consul replied. "If your clemency will—"

"Quite a crowd for a small matter," said the Emperor. "Is it a festival of some sort?"

"An exemplary punishment," the Consul said. "If your clemency—"

"Punishment? What kind of punishment?"

"A boiling in oil, which is always very popular. It is the usual punishment for presumption."

"Presumption!" Suddenly the Emperor was running up the steep walk to the Forum. The Consul and Tribune, caught by surprise, fell further and further behind as they struggled to keep up with him. He was young and they were not, and he reached the crowd long before they did. He shoved the outer parts of the crowd aside, provoking a few indelicate expressions of resentment that were quickly stifled when their authors discovered whom they were resenting. After that the purple border did its work, and the crowd parted neatly to allow the Emperor access to the main attraction.

In the middle of the Forum was a large cauldron with a fire under it, and above it an arrangement of pulleys on an arm that could be swung out over the cauldron. The executioner, a little round man with slick black hair and an immense black mustache, was supervising the tending of the fire with calm professionalism. And on a temporary wooden platform, under a sign that said "FOR PRE-SUMPTION," was Pulcheria.

"Stop this right now," the Emperor said.

The various participants gazed at him in a kind of stupor—except for Pulcheria, who was tied securely on the platform but free to use her mouth.

"Your clemency!" she cried desperately. "Is this what you meant by 'nothing bad will happen'?"

"Bring her down," the Emperor demanded, though he wasn't sure who was in charge of such things among the various gaping workmen.

By this time the Consul had caught up with him, and the Tribune was close behind. "Your clemency," said the Consul, trying his best not to puff too hard from the exertion of the hill, "it would be best not to—"

"I want her brought down from there," the Emperor told him. Now that the Consul was here, he confidently directed his attention to the one man he expected to be able to get things done.

"The difficulty," the Consul explained patiently, "is that she is suffering the appropriate punishment for a crime which, while it may—"

"She's pardoned," the Emperor declared. "I pardon her."

The Tribune, in horror, exclaimed, "You can't do that!"—which caused the Consul to cringe slightly before he recovered his usual imperturbable dignity.

"Of course I can," the Emperor said. In fact he nearly shouted it. "The Emperor grants pardons. 'Clemency' is my title. I'm granting a pardon now."

"What the Tribune means," the Consul said in his most reasonable tone, "is that it is usual, in such circumstances, to make an—"

"How many times have you brought me a prisoner to pardon? It must have been a dozen times. Only the Emperor grants pardons, you told me. Pardons are the privilege of the Emperor, you told me. Were you lying to me?"

"Of course not, your clemency. In those cases, however, the proper—"

"Then don't tell me what I can't do," the Emperor said. "That would be... It would be *presumption*," he declared with an emphatic nod toward the cauldron of boiling oil.

The Consul glanced down at the Tribune, who had turned a very unattractive shade of pale yellow. He looked back up at the Emperor, who looked quite uncharacteristically definite.

"Bring her down here," the Consul said,

After a short delay, two of the workmen ascended the platform and carefully cut the ropes that bound Pulcheria. Once she was free, she wasted no time: she ran down the wooden steps and fell on her knees in front of the Emperor. There were a few cheers from the crowd, but also some grumbling from some who were disappointed that the show was canceled.

"Oh, you don't have to do that," the Emperor said to her. "I mean, I should be begging your pardon. But it's finished now." He turned to the Consul. "Isn't it?"

The Consul was wearing his professional smile. "His clemency's word is, of course, law, although one hopes that the crowd will not be too dangerously disappointed."

"Give them something," the Emperor suggested. "Give them fried pork—you've got the oil. Fried pork for everyone this afternoon!" he called out to the crowd, and a ripple of enthusiasm rolled out from the center, producing some more definite cheers this time.

The Consul's smile was still frozen on his face; he nodded to someone, and a few men scurried away, presumably to begin the business of finding a pig.

"And now," the Consul said, "if your clemency wills it, shall we resume the expedition?"

"Of course," the Emperor replied, and the muscles in the Consul's face visibly relaxed, though the professional smile remained. "And the lady will accompany me—if, of course, she'd like to come."

"Oh!" said Pulcheria, still on her knees, but looking up now, "I don't— I mean, I wouldn't presume to—"

"The truth is I don't want to let you out of my sight," the Emperor said. "Not while there's a cauldron of oil here. It would really please me if you would be so kind as to come with me. If it's not too inconvenient for you."

"Not as inconvenient as being boiled in oil," Pulcheria replied; and when the Emperor offered his hand, she took it and rose. "Where are we going?"

"Into the Wilderness!" the Emperor replied, and he led her back down the walk from the Forum, as the crowd, now with pork on their minds, gave the pair of them a hearty cheer.

Behind them, the Tribune, his face a mask of consternation, opened his mouth to speak to the Consul; but the Consul raised one finger, and the finger was enough to enforce silence.

CHAPTER 12

THE WILDERNESS

THE HERALD, whose business was to remain impassively expressionless, displayed a slightly less impassive lack of expression when he saw a woman, and a commoner at that, walking with the Emperor; but he was too good at the heralding business to let his perfectly straight stance droop in the slightest, and he remained in the position where he had stopped when the Emperor had left the procession.

The whole parade, in fact, was frozen in place as if it had lost its motive power when the Emperor departed; many of the porters were still inside the grand passage-way, and doubtless wondering what the delay was, but certainly not saying anything, because it was not their place to say anything.

"All these people are going to the Wilderness?" Pulcheria asked almost incredulously.

"Most of them are porters," the Emperor explained.

"Good heavens! How can there be so much to port? I could carry everything I needed for a week in a basket."

"I don't think I *need* these things," the Emperor said. In almost a conspiratorial whisper, he added, "I think actually the things need me more than I need them."

"If the lady would be pleased to follow this gentle-man," said the Consul, indicating the Master of the Porters, "we can find a place for her in—"

"She can walk with me," the Emperor declared.

The Consul's professional smile remained, but his face backed away from it a little. "As your clemency wishes, of course."

And the Emperor let himself breathe again, He was defying the Consul, and he was getting away with it. This was a new sensation for him, and he was not sure yet where he stood. If Pulcheria was being punished for pre-sumption, it must mean that someone has found out about his encounter with her. And how much else?—But now he seemed to be getting his way. Was it really possible for him to get his way just by acting like...like an Em-peror?

Pulcheria, smiling uncertainly, took her place beside the Emperor in the hole in the front of the procession where he belonged, the Tribune to the left of her, the Emperor to the right of her, and the Consul to the right of him. And with its motor in place again, the procession immediately began to move, turning left into the Terrace Garden.

It was quite obvious that something was out of place at the front of the line. Everything moved with practiced precision; even the Emperor was precisely out of step. But Pulcheria, still overwhelmed by the events of the night and morning, was neither in step nor exactly out of step. She was still wearing the robes she had worn to scrub floors, and a night in a grubby cell had done them no favors. Her long black hair had mostly escaped from the loose pile she had made of it behind her head, and it flowed down her back in untidy rivulets. She was keenly aware that she was a mess. But now she was walking along one of the broad terraces of the garden, and the wonderful beauty of the place was almost making her forget her awkward position.

"A hummingbird!" she exclaimed in delight as one passed almost right in front of her on its way to some bright red trumpets blaring from a vine that dangled from the terrace above.

"The Master of the Gardens likes hummingbirds," the Emperor said. "I suppose the hummingbirds must like him, too."

"I never knew the place was so beautiful," Pulcheria said, "I heard stories, of course, but I never believed..."

"You've ever been to the Terrace Garden?" asked the Emperor. "I'm surprised. It's right off the Fountain Court. Weren't you ever curious?"

"Of course I was curious, but you *know* it's not possible for me to come in here. I mean, except by special command."

"Not possible?"

The Consul intervened. "She means, your clemency, that commoners are not allowed in the Terrace Garden."

"Really? I didn't know."

"It was not necessary for your clemency to know, since you are not a commoner."

There was something unsatisfying about that answer; but since the Emperor couldn't identify what it was, he made no reply.

The expedition had now come to the little arched bridge that crossed the stream, the one that gurgled down from the Fountain Court into the pool of St. Tryphaena down below. It was wide enough for two abreast to cross and no more, so the Herald went first, and the Emperor made it clear that he and Pulcheria were going next. The water tumbling from the terrace above made a pleasantly loud chattering sound and filled the air with cool spray, and Pulcheria stopped to admire it, with the Emperor beside her.

Finding himself next to the Consul for the moment, the Tribune risked a hoarse whisper: "This is a disaster! If——"

But the Consul's finger rose in the air again, and the Tribune knew better than to defy the finger.

After a few minutes' walk, the Terrace Garden came to an abrupt end at a thick border of bushes and trees—almost a wall of green, perhaps fifty or sixty imperial cubits high. But an arch had been cut out of the greenery straight ahead, and through it the dim and splotchy light of the forest beyond could just be seen.

Now the procession stopped, and the Herald turned and marched back along the left side of the column.

When nothing had happened for quite some tine, Pulcheria risked asking, "What's happening now?"

"We're waiting for the Guide," the Emperor replied.

"Oh," said Pulcheria.

There was silence a little while longer, except for the chattering of the birds and the whisper of a very light breeze through the leaves.

At last a wizened man with a long white beard cane trudging up the right side of the procession and took his place at the head of it. And Pulcheria had to stifle a laugh, which she was sure would not be appropriate, because the man was dressed exactly like the old Shepherd in the comedies. It was the theatrical costume exactly—the rough-cut skins, the gnarled staff, the beard, the leather boots. He was the old Shepherd, and surely his young and beautiful daughter must come along presently, pursued by the dissipated young man from the city, while her poor but virtuous shepherd swain sang his lament. Even as the long train, now under the leadership of the Guide, started to move again, Pulcheria was still waiting for the comedy to begin.

The great green gateway led into a tunnel of foliage, and then into a delightfully open forest of immense trees, many of them hundreds of years old, to judge by their girth. The shade was splattered with little puddles of sunlight here and there. Birds flitted from one tree to another, or rose in sudden bursts of panic from the dry leaves on the ground. And a guide was clearly only a ceremonial necessity, because a broad path curved along the hillside—a path that was kept scrupulously clear, and showed obvious signs of recent sweeping.

There is an awful sacredness to ancient forests, and no one was speaking as the expedition wound its way around the hillside; even footsteps were muffled by the earthen pathway, and the birds, so loquacious at the edge of the forest, had little to say here. A sighing breeze was growing louder, until it became possible to distinguish that the breeze was supplemented by another sound, growing more intense as the procession moved on. And then, after a somewhat more abrupt curve to the right, there it was, quite suddenly: a waterfall, probably twenty cubits high, plunging from a stony ledge into a pool below, from which in turn a stream flowed into a fern-banked gorge.

On the near side of the pool a gentle slope led to a plot of soft grass by the water, more natural than nature herself could have designed; flowers in white and yellow ringed the margin of it. The grassy field was broad enough to accommodate quite a large party, but it was also easy enough to imagine it—as the Emperor had often done— as the private refuge of some forest anchorite.

"Oh!" Pulcheria half-exclaimed and half-sighed. "Oh —I don't think I've ever—I know I've never seen anything so beautiful!"

The Emperor was surprised to see her wiping a tear from her cheek.

"Would you like to stop here?" he asked her.

"Yes!—I mean, of course, if your clemency—"

"We'll stop here," the Emperor declared to the Consul.

The Consul nodded and made a slight motion with his hand, and instantly there was a scrambling among the porters. Waves of men with burdens began pouring down the hill under the silent but attentive direction of the Master of the Porters, who dashed from here to there pointing at things, mostly spots on the ground. Poles rose, and great billowing masses of fabric unrolled, and there was hammering echoing from the rocks and trees, and a small city of pavilions and tabernacles rose on the grassy field with a speed that would have been incredible had it not been demonstrated in plain sight.

In a quarter-hour or less all was prepared, and the effect was gay and bright. The solemnity of the scene was gone. The Emperor led Pulcheria to the imperial pavilion, an open tent with a fabric roof bordered in imperial purple, but with no walls, and offered her a seat in an ingeniously made portable wicker armchair; he took a seat beside her, and the Consul beside him, which left the Tribune standing and looking as if he might succumb to apoplexy at any moment, since only three such chairs had been prepared for the expedition. It was not so much that he was angry as that he was out of place; he had a very definite position to occupy in these expeditions, and a cleaning-woman was sitting in it. Something like panic threatened to overwhelm him, and the only thing that kept it at bay was the Consul's finger, which occasionally rose for a moment when the Tribune appeared to be about to speak. The Consul evidently was in control, and therefore the situation could be endured.

"Do you always bring a whole city with you?" Pulcheria asked.

"It follows me," the Emperor replied. "Do you like it?"

"Oh, it's very...pleasant..."

"But you can't see the Cascade," the Emperor said. "You can't see anything but white and purple. Is that what you were thinking?"

"Not... Well, yes."

"I think it every time. I think how much I'd love to sit on the grass and dip my feet in the water and just watch the water falling. But for some reason..." He stopped and decided not to complete the thought.

"The imperial dignity, your clemency," the Consul helpfully reminded him.

"The imperial dignity," the Emperor repeated to Pulcheria.

A bowl of fruit now appeared in the hands of a servant, a little round man with slick black hair and an immense black mustache. He placed it on a small folding table, which appeared in front of the Emperor just in time through the offices of another servant; both then left the pavilion and resumed their professional invisibility.

"Peaches!" Pulcheria said with thoughtless delight; then she just as quickly recalled—her face acted out the little mental drama as broadly as if she were on the stage —that she was the guest of the Emperor and had come very close to a pot of boiling oil.

It made the Emperor smile to think how easy it would be to delight her again. "Take a peach. Take anything you like. If there were ten of me we couldn't eat it all."

Pulcheria thanked him with an expression of shy relief and took a peach, delicately, as if it might bear unexpected spines. Finding it safe, she bit into it, with a fair amount of juice running down her chin; and her expression of utter bliss was as delightful to the Emperor as the peach was to Pulcheria. He took a plum for himself; when a bit of juice dribbled on the imperial chin, a previously invisible servant appeared with a napkin to dab away the offending moisture. It had happened twice before it occurred to the Emperor that there was no one to do the same for his guest. He didn't know quite what to do about that, but eventually decided that he was getting away with quite a lot today and might dare to try it, so he took the cloth from the hand of the petrified servant and leaned over and wiped Pulcheria's chin himself. She laughed a shocked little laugh and awkwardly thanked him, swallowing a mouthful of peach. The Tribune's knees nearly buckled under him, but the raised finger of the Consul sustained him.

And since the Emperor was getting away with so

much, he decided to risk one more thing. He asked Pulcheria, "Would you like to take a walk over to the base of the Cascade? We could actually look at it from there."

"Oh, could we? I mean, if your clemency—"

"The lady and I will be taking a walk," said the Emperor, rising from his chair.

"It will be our pleasure to accompany you," the Consul replied, also rising.

"Oh, no—I wouldn't want to trouble you. The two of you can stay right here. We won't be long."

The Consul stood mute for a slightly uncomfortable length of time, and then replied, "As your clemency wishes, of course."

It took a moment after that for the Emperor to realize that he had actually won. The iron smile had not had its way: the Consul had admitted defeat. It was enough to make an Emperor feel like—like an Emperor. He offered his hand to Pulcheria, and she rose from her seat, and the two walked out of the pavilion side by side, leaving the Consul standing silent and the Tribune beginning to sputter like an overheated kettle.

"She—they—" the Tribune gasped, along with a number of less articulate syllables.

But the Consul's finger rose again, and the Tribune just barely managed to silence himself until the finger was lowered again. Then, in a low rasp, he unburdened his mind.

"Our heads are gone," he said, "Gone. We might as well sell all our hats—won't have a need for them now. Oh, I liked having a head! It isn't much, but it's the only one I've got."

"Calm yourself, my dear Tribune," the Consul said. "I

have considered the problem, and I believe I understand its nature."

"The problem is that we're going to lose our heads. The nature of the problem is sharp and steely. The S—— I mean, our patron will do it himself just for the joy of it."

"The problem, dear Tribune, is that our Emperor is a young man in the flower of youth, and we have forgotten it. He desires what all young men desire, and he has not been given it. We simply need to make arrangements to give it to him."

"But Spring Blossom After the Rain—"

"—is seven years old. All we need, you see, is a stop-gap measure. I propose a distraction."

And in the mean time, the Emperor and Pulcheria had reached the foot of the Cascade, where they sat on the grass by the water and talked about the falls, and the spray, and the ferns, and the squirrels, and really about nothing worth repeating; but if Pulcheria could read his eyes at all, she must have been aware that it was the most meaningful conversation the Emperor had ever had.

CHAPTER 13

THE MASKED BALL

"A BALL?" the Emperor asked, trying to rub his itching back against the back of the throne without being too obvious about it.

"It is arranged for tomorrow," the Consul replied.

"I don't remember knowing about it," the Emperor said, not fully concentrating on what he was saying. The purple robe always managed to be itchy in the most inaccessible place.

"It was not necessary for your clemency to know about it until now," the Consul explained with his working smile.

"What's the occasion?"

"It will be a chance for many of the senators to introduce their daughters to society," the Consul said. And then he added, with just a hint of a suggestion of an insinuation, "Their young and beautiful daughters."

"How nice for them," said the Emperor. The itch really wanted to be scratched vigorously, but he would have to twist himself into a knot to do that. "Make sure my friend Pulcheria is invited."

The smile tightened noticeably on the Consul's face.

"Unfortunately," he said carefully, "as your clemency will doubtless recall, events in the Dome are naturally restricted to the senatorial class."

"Well, that's easy to deal with," said the Emperor. "I elevate her to senatorial rank. Now there's no problem."

The Tribune began to sputter. "You—it can't—"

"The Emperor judges, sentences, pardons, elevates, and degrades," the Emperor declared. "I elevate her. What's the difficulty?'

The Consul spoke as if he were walking on pins. "The difficulty is that she has not the required substance." Seeing the Emperor's puzzled look, he added, "The money."

"She needs money?"

"As your clemency is doubtless aware, it is necessary to have a fortune of at least forty thousand sesterces to enter the senatorial class."

"If she needs money, she can have some of mine. I've got more than anybody needs. I give Pulcheria forty thousand sesterces. No, fifty thousand, so she can buy herself something nice to wear to the ball."

"Something *very* nice," the Tribune mumbled.

After a few moments of apparent consternation, the Consul resumed his accustomed serenity. "As your clemency wishes, of course."

And the Emperor thought to himself that at last he was beginning to feel like an Emperor. It was just a matter of being definite about things, of speaking with properly imperial authority. It was probably just as well that he hadn't discovered this when he was a boy, but now that he was old enough to handle it, it was a good thing to know.

"You can have the details taken care of," he continued. "A house in the senatorial quarter, properly furnished, and so on."

"Of course, your clemency." The Consul's working smile had returned, as had the look of abject dismay on the Tribune's face.

"Now what?" the Tribune asked after the audience was over and the Emperor had been sent off to his dancing-master. "It didn't work."

"His clemency posed us an unexpected challenge, it is true," said the Consul. "But all such challenges can be overcome with a certain amount of thought. If this cleaning-woman is to be there, then we must make certain that the young ladies we have in mind get to the Emperor first."

"He'll go right to her," the Tribune said stubbornly. "He'll go straight to the coarse slattern and ignore the most refined ladies we can hire."

The Consul's professional smile looked a little more devious than usual. "Not if he doesn't recognize her."

The Tribune therefore soon knew more about the ball, and the frantic preparations for it, than the Emperor knew, or ever would know if the Consul's customary care succeeded in keeping them invisible to him. It was thus something of a surprise to the Emperor when, on the evening of the ball, his valets came to dress him in a lion skin. Actually it was a cow skin with well-placed goat hair, but it looked like a lion skin.

"What's this?" the Emperor asked.

"For the ball, your clemency," the chief of the valets replied.

"Isn't it more usual to wear the imperial evening

robes?"

"It is a masked ball, your clemency."

"A masked ball?"

"Yes, your clemency, Your Clemency is to be dressed as Adrianus XVII."

"Why didn't I know this before?"

"It was not necessary for your clemency to know beforehand."

It seemed to the Emperor that it might have been at least courteous for somebody to tell him beforehand that he was going to be wearing a lion skin, although such foreknowledge could probably have done little for him. Soon he was dressed as a tolerably accurate representation of the figure of Adrianus XVII in the mosaic. He felt ridiculous. For the first time he wondered whether Adrianus XVII had felt ridiculous, too. Perhaps feeling ridiculous was the common fate of Emperors.

"Will I be wearing a mask?" the Emperor asked.

"No, your clemency," the chief of the valets replied.

"I thought it was a masked ball."

"Things are different for Emperors."

Though it was possible to enter the Dome by way of the Vestibule from the great dining-hall, the preferred way for an Emperor to make his entrance was through the ornate bronze doors that opened out on the end of the Great Colonnade. The rest of the guests had already assembled, of course, because there was no use in his making an entrance if no one was there to see it. So when he stepped in through the doors, with the Consul to his right and the Tribune to his left, the Emperor found a great assembly already gathered, all facing him to watch as he came in; and it seemed to be an assembly made up overwhelmingly of young and beautiful women. They were all wearing masks, but in compensation for covering their faces they had all chosen costumes that revealed quite a lot of the rest of them. There were Amazons and shepherdesses and Aspersian dancing-girls in swarms.

"I had no idea the senators had so many daughters," the Emperor remarked.

"They have been very productive," the Consul responded.

The imperial musicians had struck up "The Return from the Hunt," and the young ladies, and the surprisingly few older ladies and gentlemen present, applauded the Emperor's entrance. A flow of lovely girls in his direction hardly distracted the Emperor from the one thing that concerned him: he was looking out over the room, trying to see through the crowd. Was she here? Was she one of these masked beauties?

The Consul observed the Emperor's perplexity and allowed himself a smile that was less professional and more sincere than usual.

An Amazon with long legs was the first of the beauties to reach the Emperor; she made the proper obeisance in a way that suggested the possibility of all sorts of improprieties later on. About as much fabric had gone into her mask as into the rest of her costume put together. She was followed closely by a water nymph in cascading streams of gauze, and then another Amazon who did her best to live up to her role by not very subtly beating away the competition. In moments the Emperor was surrounded by feminine beauty, and the remaining guests—the young ones who had been too slow, and the older ones who had not been directed to head for the Emperor

—began to go back to whatever they had been doing, which was mostly nothing in particular.

And then suddenly the Emperor was striding briskly across the vast space under the Dome, parting waves of dancing-girls and shepherdesses in front of him and trailing nymphs and Amazons in his wake. The Consul, taken by surprise, attempted to follow, with the Tribune behind him; but the Emperor's wake closed in as the Emperor passed, and the feminine sea was turbulent and difficult to navigate.

Straight to the far side of the Dome the Emperor went, and there, just a few cubits inside the dome from the ambulatory beyond the supporting columns, was a shepherdess, to all appearances indistinguishable from any of the other shepherdesses; she was talking, or rather listening, to a senator's wife who, in spite of her faintly ludicrous costume (she was a huntress), projected an air of authority that easily came through her mask. The shepherdess had a mane of auburn hair, and her back was turned to the Emperor, but he was not fooled for a moment.

"Pulcheria!"

The shepherdess turned, and the mask that covered her eyes could not conceal the surprise in the rest of her face. "Your clemency! How did you…"

"Your shoulders," the Emperor explained with a smile. "When I first saw you—"

Suddenly an Aspersian dancing-girl was between him and Pulcheria. She made her obeisance in a way that displayed her to her best advantage, and then was joined by a wood-nymph (whose costume of well-placed leaves was appropriately woodsy) and an Amazon; and somehow it turned out that, in a very short time, he was over here, and Pulcheria was over there, with an ocean of beauties between then. The Emperor, surrounded as he was by femininity, did not see the Consul discreetly directing it all; nor did he see the Tribune indiscreetly whispering by the Consul's side. The Tribune was in a state of great agitation, and not even a raised finger could silence him now.

The Emperor was polite to all the young ladies, of course. He didn't really know how to be impolite; it had not been part of his training. But short of shoving them out of the way, which was not possible to do to a lady, there seemed to be no way to break through the feminine wall to reach Pulcheria again. Not that he was immune to the charms of the dozens of young women around him— quite the reverse, in fact. But by some quirk of the mind, or the heart, whatever desires the others roused in him only made him long all the one for the one beautiful shepherdess who seemed to be out of his reach. She might be less refined than the rest; she might be the only one whose shoulder muscles showed signs of manual labor; but for the Emperor Pulcheria was the focus of all beauty, as if all the rest of her sex were a lens through which he could discern her virtues more clearly.

And then there was dancing, which was a very formal business involving lines and intricate figures; and though there were some senators and their wives in attendance, the Emperor somehow was always surrounded by young women, not one of whom was Pulcheria.

And between the dances there were refreshments, pastries and breads and cool pink wine, all of which were brought to the Emperor by very attentive young ladies who kept asking him whether there might be anything else he would like.

It became a sort of game: the Emperor would spot Pulcheria here or there, usually being entertained, or possibly bored to tears, by some matronly senator's wife; he would head in that direction; and then a well-drilled platoon of beauties would cut him off and interpose themselves. The Emperor made more and more circuitous flanking movements to baffle then, but there were so many of them—dozens and dozens, far more than the number of senators present could account for.

And then, much to his surprise, he succeeded. He was beside Pulcheria, and the rest had not outmaneuvered him. Before anyone could interpose herself again, he took Pulcheria's hand. No one would use physical force on the Emperor.

"Would you like to go somewhere and talk?" he asked her as the platoon closed in.

"Oh— if— if it pleases your clemency—"

"Never mind me. Does it please you?"

She smiled, and the lamps all burned brighter at once. "Very much."

He led her to the door to the Vestibule, slipping past three shepherdesses, five Amazons, two wood-nymphs, three huntresses, a moon goddess, and six Aspersian dancing-girls. When the Emperor and Pulcheria walked through the doorway into the Vestibule, the others hesitated just long enough that the Emperor was able to close the door behind him.

The Vestibule was not a very inviting space for a quiet chat: it was a huge irregular room whose south wall was the outer arc of the Dome. The great dining-hall beyond it was even more forbidding: there were seats, but the table was immense, and the two lamps in the room could hardly eat up the darkness. The Emperor took one from its stand and led Pulcheria through the hall at a brisk pace, just in case any Amazons or Aspersian dancing-girls decided to pursue them. Pulcheria took off her mask to admire the shadowy magnificence around her, and then was even more amazed by the great assembly-hall beyond the dining-hall—an even less inviting space than the two before it.

"But I know just the place for us," the Emperor assured Pulcheria. "And I brought some bread."

Under the Dome, the Tribune had entered a state of near hysteria. "You're just letting him— letting him do what he wants?" he babbled to the Consul.

"He *is* the Emperor," the Consul replied.

"Since when does that mean he gets to do what he wants? Oh, I hope they don't put my head on display over the gate—at least not till I get a haircut."

"My dear Tribune, we are very far from that point. Perhaps we have failed in this attempt, but each failure is an opportunity to learn."

"What will I learn from losing my head? I can't think straight without it."

"Please do calm yourself," the Consul said. "Relax. The girls are hired through the night. Have a wood-nymph or something to calm your nerves."

The Emperor, meanwhile, had brought Pulcheria from the assembly-hall across the Arcade to the Aviary. In the dim and flickering light from the lamp he was carrying, Pulcheria could make out vines with huge leaves, and dangling flowers, and bushes that—

"Supersubstantial bread!"

Pulcheria jumped, and then she laughed when she saw Alexius the crow on a perch almost right beside her.

"Supersubstantial bread! Where's my supersubstantial bread?"

"He talks!" Pulcheria remarked with simple delighted wonder.

"Would you like to give him some bread?" the Emperor asked her. "It's the only way to shut him up." He offered her a few crumbs of bread from the leather pouch that went with his costume.

"What do I do?" she asked, taking the crumbs.

"Let him take it from your fingers. He's very gentle."

A bit timidly, Pulcheria held out a crumb between her thumb and finger. Slowly and carefully the bird leaned forward, turned his head to avoid her fingers, and closed his beak on the bread.

Once he had it, he leaned back and swallowed it down. Pulcheria laughed.

"Supersubstantial bread!" said the crow.

"He knows you have more," the Emperor explained. "He'll keep asking till it's gone."

She held out another crumb, which Alexius took as carefully as before. "He's very well trained."

"The Archeparch taught him to say that, but I taught him to eat from my hand. Every day he asks me for his bread, and every day I give it to him. Sometimes I think he's the only one in this whole vast empire who really gets what he wants from me."

"Supersubstantial bread!"

"This whole vast empire," Pulcheria repeated as if she were privately amused. And then, as Alexius took another crumb: "You're like a god to him."

"He needs his daily bread, and I give it to him. If the rest of the Empire were as simple as that, I could be one of the greatest Emperors in history."

"Supersubstantial bread! Where's my supersubstantial bread?"

Pulcheria pensively held out the last crumb. When the crow had taken it, he said no more; and so the Emperor led Pulcheria to a nearby rustic bench under a jasmine arbor. He placed the lamp on the ground in front of then. Its soft glow, the Emperor thought, made Pulcheria look far more beautiful than any of the senators' daughters. Although —

"Do you know," he said, "your natural hair is more—I mean, you look so much more yourself with black hair."

"Myself! Is that good?"

"It's delightful."

She smiled; and, pulling out a few pins, she took the wig off her head. Her own black hair cascaded over her shoulders, completely disarranged. "I felt silly with that thing on my head. And this—this shepherdess thing."

"How do you think I feel in a lion skin?"

She laughed. "Do emperors ever feel silly?!"

"Pretty much all the time."

There was a pause, filled with mutual eye-searching intense enough that the Emperor felt he really ought to find something to say.

"So... So how do you like being a senator?"

"Oh, it's— I hardly know what to do with myself. Look—I'm wearing silk! It's so thin!" (The Emperor had noticed that.) "I've never worn anything so fine before. And I've got a house with eight rooms just for me, and—

How am I going to use eight rooms? I'll have to keep getting up and moving just to use up all the rooms every day. And I've got three servants. I've got a woman who scrubs the floors! I can't believe— I just can't believe how kind you've been to me. And..."

There was an interval of silence, which the Emperor did not break because Pulcheria was obviously trying to formulate her next utterance.

"And," she continued, "I was wondering whether you wanted something from me in return."

"I do," said the Emperor. "I want you to keep telling me what you really think of me. Nobody else does that. What do I really seem like to you?"

She smiled. "Well," she began, "you're not at all what I imagined an Emperor was like."

CHAPTER 14

A MOSAIC

IN THE grand passageway just outside the Hall of Lions, the Consul was interrogating the Master of the Birds.

"*Talked?* They *talked?*"

"For hours," said the Master of the Birds.

"He came out very happy," the Consul said. "Are you quite positively sure they didn't..."

"I would have noticed. I was not that far away, and I had an excellent view."

"He didn't touch her at all?"

"I believe he kissed her hand once."

"Her *hand?*"

The great doors began to open, ending the interrogation for now.

"You did well," the Consul said, and the Master of the Birds departed looking very relieved.

The Tribune looked up at the Consul with an expression of consuming worry. "You don't suppose she told him—"

"That," the Consul replied as they stepped through the doors, "would be unthinkable."

They began the long march toward the Emperor, carefully keeping their eyes on the lions at their feet. When at last they reached the mosaic of Adrianus XVII in his lion skin, they stood with their eyes on the floor and waited.

The bronze lion began to rise, slowed, and stopped.

The Master of the Beasts stepped forward to give the thing a whack, which resounded like a gong in the vast space. But the lion did not move. The Master of the Beasts whacked it again, and then again. He whacked the lion eighteen times, but it remained stubbornly inert.

"Um... arrrr," said the Master of the Beasts.

The Consul and the Tribune looked up, and the soldiers along the walls, after a moment's hesitation, turned to face the Emperor.

"The Emperor's compliments to the Senate and the People," said the Emperor.

"The greetings of the Senate to the Emperor, the bearer of their burdens," said the Consul.

"The greetings of the People to the Emperor, the guardian of their rights," said the Tribune.

"Well," said the Emperor, "it seems to me that the first order of business is to get the lion fixed. Both of them, if we can."

"A very reasonable suggestion," the Consul agreed. "Master of the Beasts?"

"The difficulty," said the Master of the Beasts, "is that the mechanism is quite old, generations old in fact, and no one remembers how—" He noticed the Consul's expression, and decided that the proper conclusion to his speech was "But I'll see what can be done."

"Thank you," said the Consul. "And now the main business of the day. The Mosaicists' Guild has prepared a very artistic entry for your clemency's judgment. The Master of the Treasury!"

Calls for the Master of the Treasury bounced between the two rows of guards, and in a moment the man himself came through the door, followed by a large cart pushed and pulled by four men. As it rumbled across the floor (on broad wheels cushioned with felt, which made it difficult to roll but preserved the mosaic floors), the Emperor could see that it carried a large panel, a little taller than the men pushing the cart and at least three times as long as it was tall, and almost as thick as a man's arm. He could also see that the row of soldiers on his left, though many tried to maintain the fiction that their gaze was turned toward the Emperor, were actually quite taken with the panel, and seemed to be nudging one another for some reason.

When at last the cart reached the mosaic of Adrianus XVII, the men laboriously turned the cart so that the panel faced the Emperor, and he could see the pictures assembled from almost incredibly tiny colored stones.

"Good heavens," the Emperor said, stepping down from the imperial dais.

"Amorous scenes from the ancient heathen mythology," the Consul explained.

"It's very detailed," the Emperor mumbled, examining one of the scenes closely.

"A fine example of the intricate realism for which our mosaicists are justly renowned," said the Consul.

"I don't think this one is physically possible," the Emperor remarked, pointing at another one of the scenes.

"The ancients were very imaginative," said the Consul.

The Tribune said nothing: he was busy subjecting the mosaic to a close inspection.

"But is it really suitable as a gift for the Sultan?" asked the Emperor.

"The Sultan is a worshiper of Apollyon," the Consul replied. "They like that sort of thing."

"Oh, well, if they like that sort of thing... Is this a... a..." He oozed to a stop and decided not to complete the question. "Well, it's very skillful. I'm sure the Sultan would be impressed, if he likes this sort of thing."

When the audience was finished, and the Emperor had been sent off for a session with Sozomen, the Consul and the Tribune walked slowly toward the great doors with the Master of the Treasury and the mosaic rolling along beside then.

"As for *our* unfinished business," the Consul said to the Tribune, "I admit that the ball was something of a failure."

"We had the most beautiful girls money could buy, and he still chose the floor-scrubber," the Tribune remarked, shaking his head. "And then he just *talked* to her. Do you think he even knows what to do with a woman?"

"He does now," the Consul replied, glancing at the mosaic.

They walked a little while in silence.

"But perhaps you have pointed out exactly where we were wrong," the Consul remarked after some thought. "Perhaps we expected too much of him."

"What did we expect?" asked the Tribune.

"We make sure he has lessons in every subject from the best possible tutors. He has archery lessons to teach him how to shoot, dancing lessons to teach him to move gracefully, philosophy lessons to teach him what to think. But we have not given him any lessons in the amatory arts. Let a suitable young woman be found who has all the necessary skills and can give him personal instruction, step by step, and he will find that his reserve is overcome, and his natural desires satisfied; and then he will find it very easy to endure the admittedly long wait until his marriage, knowing that the means of satisfying his coarser lusts are always available to him. And then we shall hear no more of this floor-scrubber, who may be safely disposed of once his infatuation is cured."

The Tribune considered all this as they walked slowly in silence for a little while longer. At last, just as they reached the great doors, he said, "Well, I can recommend a very good wood-nymph."

If the Emperor had been privy to this conversation, he would have known why, when he retired to his chamber that evening, there was a woman in his bed.

"There's a woman in my bed," he remarked to the chief of the valets.

"Yes, your clemency," the chief of the valets replied, which was not really much of an answer to the implied question.

The Emperor looked at the woman. She was very artfully arranged on his bed, her form beautifully outlined in transparent gauze, under which was, as far as he could see, another layer of transparent gauze.

"That's not usual, is it?" he asked. He knew that it had not happened before, but he also knew that the parameters of "usual" in his life were subject to unexpected changes every once in a while.

"She is your new tutor, your clemency," the chief of the valets told him. And as the valets were continuing the process of changing him into his nightclothes, it was apparent that his new tutor was one of those who were authorized to see the Emperor undressed. He didn't know quite what to think of that, but it was usually easier to accept these things.

Once the Emperor was dressed in his imperial nightclothes, the valets made their quiet exit, and the Emperor was left alone with his new tutor.

"Well," he said, cautiously approaching the bed. Nothing else occurred to him to say.

"Please, your clemency," the woman said in a very musical voice, "come to bed with me."

"You're a...tutor?" he asked, placing one knee on the bed.

"Yes, your clemency." She took his hand and pulled just hard enough that his only choices were to get on the bed or to fall face first in her lap. "Your tutor in the arts of love." In some way she had arranged it so that he ended up sitting on the bed with her body pressed against his side.

The imperial bedchamber orchestra began to play "The Warrior and the Maiden."

"And you," the Emperor said, "—you, or—uh—are here to—"

"To teach you," she replied. She leaned back and gracefully pulled off a layer of transparent gauze, revealing a layer of transparent gauze under which was visible another layer of transparent gauze. Then she held both his hands in her own and told him, "My duty is to show you how to enjoy yourself with a suitable young lady."

"Oh," said the Emperor. He looked at the beautiful face about a hand's breadth from his own and asked, "But does there have to be music?"

She ignored that question and asked one of her own. "Do you know how to kiss a girl?"

"Of course," said the Emperor. "In theory. I've read books."

"Then we can start that way. Put your arm around my waist."

"Like this?" The Emperor tried to follow her instructions.

"Yes, but tighter. You want to be close to me."

"I do? Oh— I mean—" He tightened his grip on her waist.

"Now, when you're ready, you move your head toward the girl, and if the girl is willing, she might turn her head a little like this."

"And if she's not willing—?"

"For the Emperor, every woman is willing."

That was good to know, he supposed, though strangely unsatisfying. "So I just—" He leaned toward her a little uncertainly.

She closed the gap between them and pressed her lips to his, which was a pleasant sensation to be sure, though—

He leaned back again. "They're playing 'The Lost Shepherdess' now," he said. "Isn't the rebec a beautiful instrument?"

"That was a good first try, your clemency," the woman said, ignoring his remark about the rebec. "Now, this time, you're going to open your mouth a little and—"

"Does there really have to be music? I love music, but

I think I could concentrate on the lesson better without it."

"Let me help you concentrate," the woman said. She leaned back and pulled off a layer of transparent gauze, revealing a layer of transparent gauze under which was visible another layer of transparent gauze. Perhaps, the Emperor thought, she was just layers of gauze clean through.

"Now," his tutor said, "when our lips touch, open your mouth a little, and let your tongue play with mine for a while."

"Isn't that very—very advanced?"

"Your clemency, that's only the beginning of your lesson tonight."

"But is it right for me to— to— What I mean is, there's a lady who—"

"Yes, your clemency, and when the time comes, Spring Blossom After the Rain will be very glad you've learned to be such a good husband to her."

"Oh—yes, Spring Bl—"

Her lips were pressed to his again, and when hers moved apart he remembered to open his mouth a little, and he felt her tongue moving against his like some sort of warm serpent.

"Listen," he said, breaking away. "Do you hear how the flute doubles the rebec an octave higher? It's such a swee——"

"Your clemency," the tutor asked, trying to bring him away from the music, "what is your very deepest desire? The thing you have never told anyone about, because no one would understand?" Her lips were against his ear

now, and she told him in a breathy whisper, "I'll understand."

"Oh, well— I—" Her tongue was playing with his ear-
lobe, and the imperial bedchamber orchestra was playing
"The Lost Shepherdess" more passionately than he had
ever heard it played before. "I've always—always
thought, if only I could have just a little house in the, in
the city beyond the wall... A little—oh—one place in the
world where I could be my own man, and no one would
care that I was there, and I would walk out the door and
no one would know who I was..."

Her hand moved slowly across his chest as she whispered in his ear, "That's not the sort of desire I meant."

"Oh—then—well— Does there really have to be music?"

CHAPTER 15

THE LION-HUNT

"YOU WERE not to blame," the Consul assured the lovely young tutor. "Your skill has been vouched for by a reliable authority." (Here he glanced at the Tribune.) "Doubtless with a few more lessons, our Emperor will respond, so we shall probably have further need of your services. For now you may go."

This was a much better outcome than the poor young woman might have expected. When the Consul heard that she had been found with several layers of gauze still unremoved, and the Emperor asleep in a completely different region of the vast bed, he had been displeased. But the Master of the Emperor's Music had verified her account of her heroic struggle against his clemency's apparent indifference, and the Consul knew that his clemency could be an oddly difficult subject, and the Tribune had put in a good word for the poor woman, and in the end they could hardly blame her, could they?

"If she couldn't do it," the Tribune said when she had gone, "I don't think it can be done."

"Then perhaps we were wrong," the Consul said. "We supposed that his infatuation with his floor-scrubber was simply a matter of unsatisfied lust. But perhaps his life here has become too much of a routine. Perhaps what he saw in her was simply an escape from the regimentation of his life."

"So what do you suggest? The court ceremony must go on, you know."

"Yes. But there's no reason he can't have an occasional adventure."

Thus, in only a few hours, the Emperor found himself being dressed in the lion skin again.

"A hunt?" he asked the chief of the valets.

"Yes, your clemency. A lion-hunt in the Forest of Arches."

"But aren't lions dangerous?"

"Probably so, your clemency."

"Goodness!" But of course there was a part of him that was very excited about the prospect of a dangerous adventure. Perhaps he could never equal the martial exploits of Adrianus the Great, but he might still be a great hunter like Adrianus XVII.

The hunting-party formed at the lower end of the Arcade. The Emperor had his bow and a quiver with a dozen arrows. The Master of the Beasts explained that a lion was somewhere in the Forest of Arches; and the Emperor's goal, of course, was to shoot the beast, after which a lion-skin cloak could be made from it to memorialize the Emperor's feat. Of course the keepers of the beasts—five of them—would accompany the Emperor, but the hunt and the kill would be his alone.

The Emperor was filled with anticipation as he walked up the Arcade at the head of his party. At last he was ready to perform feats worthy of being memorialized in mosaics. Perhaps one day the Hall of Lions would have a mosaic of him delivering the fatal arrow to his leonine foe. He quickened his pace up into the Forest of Arches.

It was a different place in the daylight. The weather was pleasantly warm without being hot; the sky was overcast with an even layer of lightly textured clouds, so that the day was bright without sun and shadows. There was no wind, which was a very good thing: the Emperor had enough experience shooting at targets to understand how to compensate for the wind, but it was just as well not to have to worry about wind when the target was a terrible beast. The gardens were a tapestry of well-chosen colors carpeting the chambers of the ancient ruins; here and there birds chanted at the tops of the arches; bees buzzed on their very important errands; and above those sounds the Emperor could hear his own heart beating. Somewhere in here was a ravening monster, and just by existing it turned the familiar landscape into a world of epic and romance.

Where would you be if you were a lion? The Emperor strode quickly across the great open space of the ancient basilica. Certainly not here: there was no cover, and a hunted beast would hide. So would a hunting beast, he thought quite suddenly, and it gave him a thrill to realize that he might be as much hunted as hunter. His step quickened even more; he was well ahead of the rest of the party, some of whom were half-jogging to keep up with him. He reached the hall of reliefs several paces ahead of the fastest of the keepers.

From any of these ancient doorways a lion might spring. The Emperor had his bow ready. He ought perhaps to have moved cautiously from one doorway to another, but he was not in a mood for caution. He was half-jogging now himself. And it occurred to him halfway down the hall of reliefs that the next doorway led to a very suitable place for a lion to hide. He made a sudden right turn, bow at the ready, into the ancient baths.

That was what the antiquarians called them, and they were probably right. Here was a great open space with several sunken rectangular pits, now turned into lush garden plots with morning glories tumbling down the sides. In any of these the lion might try to hide among the dense plantings, but woe betide him if he did, for the Emperor was ready to send an arrow through him from above.

No lion appeared, however, and the Emperor's cautious search gave the keepers of the beasts time to catch up with their master. He was strangely disappointed by their arrival, and realized that their presence would somehow diminish his accomplishment when he killed the lion. He had been imagining them coming upon a mosaic-ready scene of him standing over the carcass of the beast, bow in hand. Now he started to think how easy it would be to lose the rest of the party in the labyrinth.

Finding no lions in the baths, the Emperor continued through to the library, as he liked to think of it: it was full of remains of inscriptions in the ancient epic dialect, which the antiquarians had identified as quotations from the ancient heroic poems, some of which were otherwise lost. There were not very many places for a lion to hide in here, so the Emperor accelerated, and once again began to leave his followers behind him.

A roofless corridor led out of the library, a corridor once lined by small cells or rooms, most of them now only

outlines of foundations. Had it been a dungeon? Some antiquarians thought so, but the Emperor sided with the
ones who thought them the cells of heathenish priests or
monks who tended the library.

The wails had mostly vanished here, leaving little shelter for a concealed lion, so the Emperor rushed through
—he was nearly running now—on his way to the end of
the corridor. And was that a movement up there? He persuaded himself that it was, and he put on more speed as
he reached the most labyrinthine part of the labyrinth.

Here, though it was (said the antiquarians) the most
ancient part of the ancient ruins, the walls were more substantial and still stood above a man's height in most
places. This section was a series of interconnected chambers of various sizes, each connecting to one or more
other chambers, with no corridors running through: apparently the idea of corridors had not yet occurred to the
most ancient of the ancients. The Emperor knew his way
through this maze, and he knew that the keepers of the
beasts did not. He lost them at once, even though he
paused at each doorway to see whether a pouncing lion
awaited him. No lion appeared, however, and as he
twisted his way through the chambers by the only route
that led to the other side, he began to hear the keepers of
the beasts calling to him. Let them call, he thought with
a slightly wicked amusement that he would certainly
have to confess to the Archeparch later. They'd find
their way out eventually, and meanwhile the glory of the
kill would be his alone. Wouldn't it be splendid to describe the mighty combat to Pulcheria?

After many turns that were sure to baffle the rest of

the party, he emerged beside the row of freestanding columns—

And then he heard it: an unmistakable bellow, the roar of the horrid beast. The sound led him to turn into the series of interconnected chambers with fallen roofs covered with morning glories. He heard it again, much closer. More cautiously now he advanced into the next chamber, and then the next, and then he saw it.

It was in the little half-roofed room that was his nightly destination when the moon was bright, and it was just leaping up on the altar.

The Emperor raised his bow and walked slowly forward. The lion saw him, but it did not attack. Instead it lay on the stone like a sacrificial victim awaiting its fate. It was a magnificent beast, with a lush mane that would nicely decorate its skin when—

And then the Emperor lowered his bow.

The lion was chained. A thick iron chain led from the beast's neck, where presumably a collar of some sort was buried in all that fur, to a stout stake driven into the ground.

This was not a hunt at all. It was meant to be a simple slaughter. The lion had no chance to escape, no chance to defend himself.

The Emperor looked at the beast on the altar, and the beast looked back at him. They understood each other, or so it seemed to the Emperor. He was sure that the lion had no fear of him. He laid his bow and arrow on the ground and slowly approached the reclining beast, his hand open and turned upward. He came close enough to look into the lion's great dark eyes and see his own reflection.

Then the lion's huge front paw came at him.

For just a moment the Emperor froze in fear. But the paw touched him gently on the chest.

The Emperor looked down at the huge paw, and then carefully touched it with his hand. The lion seemed to approve.

"You've got no claws," the Emperor said softly. He let the paw go and gently reached toward the lion's neck: he stroked the lush mane, and felt the heavy collar under it. "You're tame, aren't you? You're a tame, chained, clawless beast." He laughed quietly. "You're just like me." And the Emperor was surprised to find that there was a bit of a tear in his eye. He gently scratched around the lion's collar, and the lion closed his eyes in contentment. With his great leonine head he gently nudged and rubbed against the Emperor's chest. He liked to be petted.

The Emperor felt a dull despairing anger welling up inside him. They had meant to give him an adventure, but it would be no adventure at all. They had made sure there would be no danger, and therefore no accomplishment. They had simply planned to sacrifice a harmless and innocent beast—this magnificent animal, with his warm fur and his shining dark eyes, this creature who meant no one harm and was capable of love.

"They won't hurt you," the Emperor said softly as the lion affectionately rubbed against him. "I won't let anyone hurt you. I don't know whether the Emperor has any power at all, but if I have, you're under my protection. They'll have to go through me to get to you."

And at that moment the keepers of the beasts finally found their way to the Emperor, or perhaps guessed that he had found his way to the chained lion. They came in and stopped suddenly at the dropped bow. They tried to understand the scene that presented itself to their eyes.

"The lion-hunt is over," the Emperor told them with a smile. "I found the lion."

CHAPTER 16

JEROME

THE Master of the Beasts had seemed curiously evasive when the Consul and the Tribune questioned him about the hunt. Yes, in general, he had said, it could certainly be called a success. The Emperor seemed very pleased, and that was the main thing. As for the details, well, yes, of course he would fill those in later, but wasn't it time for him to be taking up his position in the Hall of Lions? Oh, dear, yes it was. And he hurried off toward the passage that led around to the back of the hall.

The Consul was curious about those details, but if the Emperor had enjoyed himself, then perhaps they had found what he needed. As he made the long march through the Hall of Lions, his eyes on the floor, he walked with a steady and optimistic pace, which meant that the Tribune had to stretch his strides out a little more than usual to keep up with him.

When they reached the mosaic of Adrianus XVII, there was a deep and resonant roar.

"Ah!" the Consul remarked. "The lion's been repaired. Very—"

He froze and fell silent.

A lion was sitting beside the Emperor on the imperial dais. The Emperor was absentmindedly scratching the lion's head with his right hand, as if—as if Emperors scratched lions' heads every day.

"The lion-hunt was a success," said the Emperor happily. "I found the lion." He thought it was a fine joke, and it would have been a shame if the Consul and the Tribune had not had a chance to hear it. In his delight in his new lion friend, he had overcome his resentment of the staged hunt.

The Consul and the Tribune stared mutely at the lion.

"His name is Jerome," the Emperor continued. "Isn't that a splendid name for a lion?"

"Splendid" was the only word the Consul could produce at the moment.

"He's very gentle," the Emperor said. "Why don't you come closer and meet him?"

The Consul looked down at the Tribune. The Tribune looked up at the Consul. Then the Tribune turned and sneezed. A sneeze from the Tribune was something of an event: it resonated and echoed up and down the great hall for some time.

When the echoes died down, the Consul turned back to face the Emperor. "Meet the lion?"

"He likes people," said the Emperor.

"Doubtless," the Consul replied with a very doubtful expression.

"And he's got no claws," the Emperor added, hoping to sound encouraging.

Looking like a man resigned to his fate, the Consul slowly approached. But he had taken only a few steps when the lion suddenly stood with a roaring growl even louder than the Tribune's sneeze. Baring his teeth, Jerome interposed himself between the Consul and the Emperor. He did not move to attack in any way: he simply made sure that the path to the Emperor lay through the lion.

"I'm sorry about that," the Emperor said. "He seems to think he needs to protect me. It's all right, Jerome. The Consul is a good man."

Jerome, however, plainly indicated that he would be the judge of that.

The Consul stepped back, and Jerome seemed satisfied with that gesture.

The Tribune sneezed again, which attracted Jerome's attention. The lion walked down from the dais and straight toward the Tribune, who stood frozen, not at all sure what to do about an approaching lion. Jerome might not have claws, but he had teeth enough. He had displayed then, white and sharp, very prettily for the Consul.

When Jerome reached the Tribune, however, he rubbed his great head affectionately against the Tribune's hips, nearly toppling him. The Tribune sneezed.

"He likes you," said the Emperor.

"How delightful," said the Tribune. He sneezed again, a great roaring sneeze.

"Perhaps the Tribune speaks his language," the Consul said when the echoes of the sneeze had died down.

Jerome turned and rubbed the other side of his whole body along the Tribune's hip. The Tribune sneezed again, and Jerome let out a happy little roar.

"Goodness," said the Emperor. "Are you feeling all right, Tribune?"

"Cats have this effect on me."

"Oh, I'm sorry. Perhaps you'll get used to him." The Tribune sneezed again.

"Jerome, come here," the Emperor called, patting the arm of his throne; and, in a very uncatlike way, Jerome responded immediately, jumping back up on the dais and resuming his position by the Emperor's side.

"He isn't going to make a mess in here, is he?" the Consul asked. He had addressed his question to the Master of the Beasts, but the Emperor answered before anyone else had a chance to speak.

"Oh, no. He's marvelously well trained. He does his business in a sand pit. Won't do it anywhere else."

The Tribune sneezed.

After the echoes had subsided, the Emperor remembered, "Oh! We didn't do the greetings. The Emperor's compliments to the Senate and the People."

Without delay, the Consul replied, "The greetings of the Senate to the Emperor, the bearer of their burdens."

The Tribune replied with a resonant sneeze that was accepted as his contribution to the ceremony.

"Now," said the Emperor, "what is the business of the day?"

"An entry for your clemency's judgment from the Guild of Glassblowers and Engravers," the Consul replied.

"Oh! Well, let's see it. What do you think, Jerome?"

Jerome seemed to be thinking only of how much he liked to have his head and mane scratched. His eyes were closed, and his head was tilted toward the scratching hand. The Consul decided not to wait for the lion to render his opinion, and called out,

"The Master of the Treasury!"

This initiated the usual series of calls that brought in the Master of the Treasury. He was followed this time by a man carrying a small stand, and behind him two men with a very large bowl between them. They moved slowly and carefully, which gave the Tribune time to get four more sneezes in, as well as a fair amount of sniffling.

When the Master of the Treasury came to the front of the hall at last, he bowed. He took no apparent notice of the lion: perhaps he had been warned about it, or perhaps his imperturbable nature simply accepted the lion with the assurance that it was not the Master of the Treasury's place to deal with any animals introduced to the imperial court. The stand was set up, and the bowl placed on it—a great glass bowl four cubits across, engraved with pictures remarkable for their fine detail.

The Emperor stepped down to examine the bowl, and Jerome stood and followed him.

"Lion-hunting scenes," the Emperor said, looking closely at the engravings. Jerome rubbed affectionately against his hip.

"Yes, your clemency," said the Consul. The Tribune was doing his best to hold in another sneeze.

Jerome rubbed himself against the stand. It rocked, and the bowl nearly toppled, but the Master of the Treasury steadied it.

"I don't think Jerome likes lion-hunting scenes," the Emperor said with a smile.

"Perhaps not," the Consul said as Jerome rubbed the whole length of his body against the Emperor, "but it is not the lion's opinion that is being solicited."

Jerome turned to rub the other way; his tail whipped

around and struck the bowl with a musical clong, but the porters were ready and steadied the bowl again.

At that moment the Tribune lost the battle with his sneeze, which erupted with explosive force. When his eyes opened, there was a puddle of shattered glass where the bowl had been.

For a moment the men all stared at the ruins in silence. The Emperor was the first to speak;

"Insufficiently rare and exquisite?"

The Consul nodded, and the Tribune looked relieved.

"Come on, Jerome," the Emperor said, turning and mounting the dais again. "We don't want you to hurt your paws." And the lion happily followed him.

"No," the Consul repeated quietly. "We don't want that."

Seating himself on the throne again, the Emperor asked, "Is there any other business for today?"

The Consul stepped out of the way of the swarm of servants who had already descended on the wreckage of the bowl. "No, your clemency."

"Well, I have one," the Emperor said, which was quite surprising to the Consul and the Tribune. The Tribune was busy sneezing, but when the echoes died down both he and the Consul looked up at the Emperor with genuine curiosity.

"I'd like to invite my friend the lady Pulcheria to have dinner with us. If she wishes to, of course."

The Consul looked down at the Tribune, but the Tribune was considering the possibility of another sneeze and therefore had no contribution to make.

"Very good, your clemency," the Consul said, suppressing his expression of resignation.

"Do you think she'll come?" the Emperor asked with boyish eagerness.

"She will come," the Consul replied. "The Emperor's word is law."

And indeed Pulcheria did come. It was a matter of some concern to the Consul that there was so little time to prepare her, but she was dressed as presentably as she could be and given a few brief instructions in imperial court etiquette for dinner, and that would have to do.

She had not, however, been warned that a lion might be present at the dinner. Perhaps the Consul and the Tribune had not expected that the Emperor would invite his feline guest to dinner, or perhaps they hoped Pulcheria might make a fool of herself by screaming "Eek! A lion!"—But in either case they were mistaken.

"A lion!" Pulcheria exclaimed with unalloyed delight when the Emperor and Jerome came into the dining-hall. For the moment she had completely forgotten the etiquette lesson she had received earlier in the afternoon.

Nor was the Emperor any more mindful of etiquette. "Pulcheria! Why are you all the way down here? Come here and meet Jerome. There's a place for you right beside me."

The Consul, doing his best to seem unruffled, said in a low voice, "That seat is traditionally reserved for the Empress."

"Yes," said the Emperor, "but it's empty for the next nine years. We'll be done with dinner before then." He was feeling very imperial today: he was learning that he could have everything his way if he just assumed that there was no other possibility.

Pulcheria, looking like a woman who was very much

aware of the eyes of all the other guests on her, walked the considerable length of the table up to its head, making as little sound as possible with each step. But the Emperor's welcoming smile when she reached him earned a smile from her in return.

"This is Jerome," the Emperor told her. "We had a lion hunt, and I found the lion." He would probably never tire of that joke.

"He's beautiful," she said.

"He's very friendly," the Emperor assured her, and as if to demonstrate the truth of that assertion, Jerome nudged Pulcheria with the top of his head, nearly knocking her off balance. She laughed.

"He likes it when you scratch the top of his head," the Emperor said "Especially behind the ears."

Pulcheria tried the experiment, and Jerome closed his eyes in simple and perfect contentment.

"He's so soft," she remarked. The Tribune sneezed.

Pulcheria was seated on the Emperor's left, with the Tribune to her left; the Consul was in his usual place at the Emperor's right. Jerome tolerated him there unless he made any kind of sudden movement toward the Emperor; then Jerome gave him a low growl, which was always enough to correct the situation to his satisfaction.

The Emperor thought Pulcheria looked beautiful dressed as a fine lady, but then he thought she had been beautiful dressed as a floor-scrubber, too. He delighted in having her next to him; he delighted in her delight at his new lion friend; he delighted in being in control at last and having things his way. Jerome took a simpler delight in being among friends who dropped bits of meat on the floor for him.

Neither the Consul nor the Tribune enjoyed the dinner quite as much. The Tribune did his best to limit his sneezing, but he still sneezed once every two or three minutes. Between sneezes he produced undignified snorting sounds. The Consul, for his part, was never allowed to forget that he was under a watchful leonine eye.

Nor did the rest of the guests demand much of the Emperor's attention that afternoon. They were honored to have been invited to his table, as always, but they were not inclined to ask anything special of him when there was a lion loose in the dining-hall.

As the dinner came to an end, the Emperor realized that it would mean the end of his time with Pulcheria as well. And since he did not want his time with her to end yet, he summoned up the courage to ask her the question that had been on his mind all through dinner:

"Lady Pulcheria, will you take a walk with me in the Forest of Arches?"

And he held his breath until she answered, "Oh, yes, thank you, I'd love to go!"

"It will be our pleasure to accompany you," the Consul said automatically.

"No need to trouble yourselves," the Emperor said. "I know the way."

After a moment of awkward silence, the Consul reluctantly replied, "As your clemency wishes, of course."

The Tribune sneezed.

And Pulcheria asked, "Can your lion come with us?"

CHAPTER 17

THE TOWER OF DIOTREPHES

THE sun was low, casting golden light on the standing arches and columns and long shadows in the spaces between them. Jerome the lion instantly found a bed of creeping thyme in the great open garden at the entrance to the Forest of Arches, and he rolled in it with simple feline delight. The Master of the Gardens would probably not be pleased, but it would give him something to do in the morning.

"I've heard so many stories about this place," Pulcheria said as she looked around her at the great ancient basilica, with sky for a ceiling and bits of ancient mosaic floor still showing between the lush garden plots. "Is it true that you can get lost in here and never find your way out? That's what they say about it."

"It's not that big," the Emperor assured her. "You could get lost for a while, but you'd get out eventually. If nothing else, you always know where the Tower of Diotrephes is, because you can see it from almost everywhere. And besides, you can't get lost when you're with me." He held out his hand, and she took it very naturally, and the Forest of Arches had never seemed more like paradise to him.

Jerome was happy, too. He explored and enjoyed the gardens, but he never allowed more than a few dozen paces to separate him from his people, and he certainly never allowed them out of his sight. If they stopped to admire a patch of coreopsis or smell the mignonette, he presented himself for some scratching of the head and mane, which was never refused him.

When they entered the hall of reliefs, Pulcheria was fascinated by the carvings, where long-forgotten battles known only to students of the ancient epics were memorialized in slowly eroding stone. "All these ancient warriors," she said—"can they really be gone? You hear stories about ghosts in this place. Everyone says it's haunted. They say that's why no one goes in after dark."

"I'm absolutely sure there are ghosts," the Emperor said. With his free hand he was scratching behind Jerome's ear, and the tilt of Jerome's head and the expression of utter bliss on his face were good indications that behind the ear was precisely where lions needed to be scratched.

"Really?" asked Pulcheria. "You don't think that's just a silly superstition?"

"I've seen them."

"Seen them?" She sounded very surprised.

"I'll tell you my secret," he said as they began strolling again. "I've often been here at night. I come here in the moonlight, you see. It's the most beautiful place in the world in the moonlight. No one knows I come out here—"

"Oh!—That's what you were doing the night you came into the pantry!"

"Yes, it was. The luckiest night of my life." He felt a little more pressure from her hand as he continued, "And I've seen the ghosts. I think so, anyway. I see figures moving between the shadows sometimes. But they never do me any harm. I think they must be wandering here because they can't bear to leave the place."

By this time they had reached the atrium, which the Master of the Gardens had planted as a tapestry of purples and yellows. Jerome was sniffing at the thyme borders: he seemed to be fond of thyme. He experimentally chewed a few sprigs of the stuff.

"Oh, I can see why," said Pulcheria. "If I had to be a ghost, this is where I'd choose to wander for eternity. Eternity wouldn't be too much time to enjoy this place."

"There's one particular part of it I wanted to show you," the Emperor told her.

They walked through the atrium by way of the artistically winding path that led through the center of it. Turning right at the other side, they followed the line of orphaned columns, their capitals gilded by the evening sun; and then left into the series of vaulted chambers, where the mounds of rubble that had once been roofs were covered with morning glories, their pink and violet flowers tightly rolled in preparation for tomorrow's display.

At last they reached the little half-roofed chamber with the altar, and the Emperor announced, "This is the place."

Pulcheria looked around her, and the Emperor saw the chamber through her eyes. The Master of the Gardens had put a few patches of toadflax in the sunnier parts, and the back wall, under the roof, was covered with ivy, whose leaves danced a vertical ballet as puffs of evening breeze rolled into the chamber and found themselves trapped. It was all pretty, but it would be hard for anyone else to see why it was the Emperor's destination.

Looking up at the remainder or the roof, and the walls with their fluted pilasters, Pulcheria sat on the stone altar. Jerome, whose appetite for affection could not be sated, rubbed himself against her legs. If he had any memory of being chained here, he had forgiven everyone.

"What is this place?" Pulcheria asked.

"They say it's the inner chamber of a heathen temple," the Emperor told her. "That would have been the altar where they made their sacrifices."

"Sacrifices! What kind of sacrifices?"

"Probably virgins," the Emperor said mischievously.

"Oh," said Pulcheria, looking a little relieved.

"But that's not why I come here." Somehow Jerome's ear had ended up under his hand again, so he was scratching behind it as he told her, "I come here to imagine that I'm not me."

"Who do you imagine you are?" she asked with a smile.

"Nobody. That's the point of it. I come here to imagine that I'm nobody special—not an Emperor, not a Consul, not a senator, just a man. A man who has his own little house, and when he comes through the door into his house, he's home, and no one needs him to do anything or be anything, because no one even knows who he is, and no one cares. That's what I'd really like to be: someone nobody cares about. Except— except I think it might be nice if *one* person cared."

Pulcheria let this remark pass without any other comment than an encouraging smile.

"And this is where I found Jerome, too," the Emperor
continued. He decided not to add any more details, since
he was still a little angry when he thought about the lion-
hunt, and he also felt as if someone had made a bit of a
fool of him. "This is where I come to sit and be alone, but
it does seem much more pleasant with you here."

With an even more encouraging smile, she replied, "I
almost wish we could stay here and not go back."

The Emperor took her hand again, which meant that
the scratching behind Jerome's ear stopped. The lion
looked up and saw that the two humans had stopped paying attention to him. It could be tolerated for a short
while. He flopped down on his side and expressed a little
impatience with his tail. All they were doing was looking
at each other, and was there any good reason why someone could not be scratching a lion's ear at the same time?

After a long and searching look, the Emperor spoke
again in a lower voice. "We should get going so we don't
end up in here after dark. With no light, you see... But I
thought... I thought you might like to go see the sunset
with me."

Pulcheria said that would be a delightful thing to do.
And Jerome was in favor of moving again. As soon as the
people began to walk, he was on his feet padding after
them.

Ascending the slope through more chambers and
courts of the ancient ruins, they came at last to the upper
extremity of the Forest of Arches. And there, walking
out through the north gate, they found themselves on the
slope of the Eminence. Above them loomed the Tower of
Diotrephes, huge and impossibly tall, standing straight

and rigid on the peak of the Eminence. Its western side was bathed in yellow-orange sunlight, and it cast a shadow right across the senatorial quarter to the east and on out over the Narrows.

The Emperor led the way up the steep slope to the base of the tower—and the base was quite a structure in its own right. It had the look of a mausoleum, all heavy square stone with small windows and a narrow door. The tower sprouted from the top of this massy cube, with narrow windows all the way up to a parapet at the top.

"I've never been up here before," Pulcheria remarked as they reached the base of the tower. She was breathing a little heavily from the climb, as was the Emperor himself. (Jerome had bounded up the hill with no visible effort.)

"Really?" the Emperor responded. He was about to ask why she hadn't been up here, but then he remembered the reason. There were many places not permitted to commoners, and this must be one of them. "Well, here we are now. It's the highest point in the palace grounds, and we can see everything from here. Look—down there is the Narrows, and you can see the sunlight on the Sultan's palace across the water. It must be a beautiful place, with all those domes and spindly tower things. Our most loyal vassal deserves a beautiful place to live in, after all."

"I suppose he does," Pulcheria said quietly. Then, a bit more sure of herself, she asked, "What's inside the tower?"

"We can go in and see," the Emperor replied. "We still have a little while before the sun sets."

The entrance was a narrow door on the sunny west side. The guard on duty, a little round man with slick black hair and an immense black mustache, was of course happy to let the Emperor and his companions in; nor did he seem at all worried that one of them was a lion.

Inside was dim, but with a streak of golden light pouring in through the door. A narrow stairway wound up the inside of the tower, and shafts of sun shot in like arrows through the narrow windows on the west side.

"Look," said Pulcheria—"you can go all the way up. Have you ever been up to the top?"

"No," the Emperor answered. "I'd be afraid of ending up like poor old Diotrephes."

"Diotrephes? Did he come to a bad end?"

"That's why the tower is named for him."

"I thought he was the one who built the tower."

"No, that was...some Adrianus or other. Diotrephes is the one who died here. You don't know the story?"

She assured him that she didn't.

"It's a famous love story. There's a play about it. He was in love with someone, and he couldn't marry her, you see, and so he threw himself off the tower and died. I mean, of course he died, because people don't fall from heights like that and live."

"Oh! That's so sad! The poor man."

"There's a lot more to the story, of course. I don't tell it very well. You should see the play—it's the most beautiful play I've ever seen. We have it in the library, too, if you'd like to read it."

"I'd... well, I...don't read."

"Oh. Well, we'll have the play performed soon. But now it's time for the best show we have, even better than the play. There's nothing like a sunset from the Eminence when the clouds are just right."

And the clouds were just right. They had been puffs of white all afternoon, but now, as the Emperor and his two companions came out the narrow little door, they were already burning orange, their sunward edges blazing. The Emperor sat on the grass with Pulcheria beside him, and Jerome flopped down beside her, his head in a convenient scratching position.

The sun touched the horizon, deepening to red, and the clouds burned with oranges and reds and magentas, as if someone had set the sky on fire. As the sun vanished, the colors deepened, and the landscape darkened, and it seemed quite natural for the Emperor to take Pulcheria's hand and bring it to his lips; and of course that caused her to look at his eyes instead of the western sky; and in another moment he realized that her head was tilting a little, which was a sign he had been taught to look for. And when he moved his lips toward hers, she was indeed very willing.

Jerome the lion felt the absence of the scratching hand and looked up. But the people were occupied, and the grass was soft, and he laid his head down and waited patiently for someone to notice the lion again.

The colors faded far too fast. The last hints of deep rose were still lingering as Pulcheria rested her head on the Emperor's shoulder, and for a long time they wordlessly watched the dying light, until nothing but dull grey twilight was left.

Then at last the Emperor said, "I suppose we should be going back. But it was a beautiful sunset."

"It was the most beautiful sunset there ever was," Pulcheria agreed, pressing her cheek into his shoulder. "Oh, why does everything beautiful have to end?"

CHAPTER 18

THE EMPEROR'S CONCUBINE

CONFESSION came easily this time. The Emperor wasn't at all sure which of the things on his mind were sinful, but he did have a lot of things he wanted to talk about.

First he mentioned his evening with the love-tutor, because he thought that might have been a thing to confess. The Archeparch assured him that, although for ordinary men a night spent with a harlot might count as a minor sin, of not much account but perhaps worth an Our Father or two, for an Emperor it was a reasonable and in a certain sense laudable means of satisfying the lusts of the flesh, so that they did not stand in the way of his imperial duties. The Archeparch did ask him to recount the evening in detail, so as to allow a more precise determination of the sinfulness of the individual actions involved, and he seemed quite disappointed to learn that there were very few details to recount. "But didn't you tell me last time that you had impure thoughts?"

"I do have impure thoughts," the Emperor insisted. "It's just that these past few days they've mostly been about my friend Pulcheria."

"Is she the harlot?"

"No! She's a lady. She's the only person in the world who cares about me. Everyone else cares about the Emperor, but she cares about *me*. And it makes me... It makes me think of doing things with her."

"Do you imagine her without her clothes?"

"Often," the Emperor replied, not looking the Archeparch in the eye.

"What does she look like?"

"I think she's the most beautiful woman I've ever seen. She has long black hair, and her eyes are the most beautiful brown, like brown gemstones, and when she smiles at me I think she must be an angel."

"How about her legs?" the Archeparch asked. "Have you seen her legs?"

"Well, yes, when she was dressed as a shepherdess. It was very short, the shepherdess thing she was wearing, and very thin..."

"And were her legs like...alabaster pillars?" the Archeparch asked with keen interest.

"More sort of brown, I'd say."

"Pity. I prefer alabaster pillars. But I don't see any real harm in it. You find this woman more to your taste than the harlot. There is no need to worry about your impure thoughts. Simply translate your impure thoughts into deeds, and the thoughts will no longer trouble you. Have the woman brought to you and have your way with her, and think no more of it."

"No!" The Emperor surprised himself with his vehemence and deliberately moderated his voice when he continued. "I mean, the trouble with my impure thoughts is that they seem so...so pure. I don't want to *make* her do what I want. I want her to *want* to do what I want.

Otherwise I don't want it."

The Archeparch looked slightly shocked. "Your clemency, that sounds almost like love."

"Is that bad?"

"Your clemency, love is not a relation proper to Emperors. Emperors make marital alliances to strengthen their position among their vassals, as your betrothal to the Sultan's daughter has done. For the indulgence of their natural humors, they have resort to harlots and concubines and such expedients. But love is apt to cloud a ruler's thoughts and interfere with the administration of the Empire."

The Emperor was looking down at the floor and slightly to his right. "It's a serious sin, then?"

"I think it may warrant *four* Our Fathers," the Archeparch replied gravely. Then, more cheerfully: "Get them out of the way before the liturgy, and you're absolved."

The Emperor loved the liturgy as always, though his happiness was mitigated a little by the sense that, once again, he had not really been able to repent of anything. He wasn't sure what he ought to be repenting of. The Archeparch had told him that love was the most serious sin he had confessed, but it didn't feel like a sin at all. He hadn't called it love before, but now that the word had been presented to him, it seemed a perfect description of what he had felt when Pulcheria was beside him, and what he felt now when he wished she could be beside him. Even his physical desire for her expressed itself as an overwhelming desire that she would desire him. As much as it had shocked the Archeparch, that felt very pure and good. Something weighed on his conscience, but that was not it.

After the liturgy, the Emperor spent some time in the Fountain Court with some of his courtiers, as usual, while the Consul and the Tribune had a frustrating conversation with the Archeparch.

"Yes, we know all about this infatuation of his," the Consul said testily after a particularly elaborate and difficult series of gestures from the Archeparch. "He kissed her on the Eminence last night, our informants tell us. And then he brought her down and had her escorted back to her house. It's disgusting. If he'd ravished her on the spot, that would have been appropriately imperial behavior at least, but instead he's acting like a common schoolboy. He went to bed alone last night, except for that horrid lion—he insisted on having the beast with him. Do you know he's had one of the imperial vestries turned into a sand-pit?"

"I did suggest a harlot," the Archeparch pointed out, so that it was clear that none of this was strictly speaking his fault. "Or a concubine."

The Tribune shook his head. "We asked him if he wanted the wood-nymph back for a second lesson. He just said, 'Not tonight.'"

"And as for a concubine," the Consul began— And then he stopped.

"As for a concubine," he repeated much more slowly... "As for a concubine, it might solve all our problems."

"We can't make him take a concubine," the Tribune objected. "He just won't. If the wood-nymph couldn't do it, no one can. He's just too infatuated with this floor-scrubber."

"He'll take a concubine," the Consul said, "because the concubine will *be* the floor-scrubber."

"But—" the Tribune sputtered. "But— but——" He seemed to be stuck.

"Forget for the moment that she is entirely unsuitable as a companion for our young Emperor. Forget that he has forced her on us in spite of our most careful precautions. Consider the problem as a logical one. The difficulty this unfortunate infatuation presents is that there is no place for a floor-scrubber in the imperial court except *qua* floor-scrubber, and the Emperor has been forcing her into places where she does not belong. But there is a traditional place for concubines. They warm the imperial bed, and they satisfy the imperial lusts, and they are discreetly kept at the service of the Emperor, who therefore has no need to try to make respectable ladies of them in order to enjoy their companionship. Let our Emperor take this woman as a concubine for as long as he likes until the Sultan's daughter is of age. Let him keep her after that if he desires it, for what has marriage to do with pleasure? But I expect him to tire of her in a month or two."

"I think it would be a disaster," said the Tribune gloomily.

"My dear Tribune, you are simply failing to see things from a practical point of view. I share your distaste for the woman, but it is not my bed she is going to infest. I do not have to share our Emperor's unorthodox notions of beauty. The woman does not have to appeal to me."

"Yes, but the Sultan's daughter—"

"The Sultan's daughter will be available in nine years. If he loves her, well and good. If he is indifferent to her, it makes no difference. The Emperor will still be a young man; he should be vigorous enough to produce an heir even under adverse circumstances. I think we have found the solution to our problems, and I only regret that we did not think of it sooner."

The Tribune grumbled, but finally turned to the Archeparch. "Well, what do you think?"

"It will certainly make his confessions more entertaining," said the Archeparch.

And so the matter was settled. All that remained was to inform the Emperor of the decision and make him believe it was his own. And that could doubtless be easily accomplished.

It was accomplished along the Great Colonnade, which the Consul had suggested to the Emperor as a suitable place to discuss a somewhat delicate personal matter.

"It has not escaped our attention," the Consul began when the time had come to discuss the delicate personal matter, "that your clemency has spent some considerable time with the Lady Pulcheria in the past few days."

"And I'll probably spend more," the Emperor said a little warily. He was ready to endure an oration on her unsuitability as a companion, but he was certain it would not change his mind.

"Since we, of course, have no other wish than your clemency's happiness, which we regard as essential to the prosperity of the Empire," the Consul continued, "we simply wish to make it clear to ourselves in what relation to your clemency we are to perceive the lady. Your clemency's will, as always, is law."

"If my will is law, then I plan on seeing a lot more of her."

"Very good, your clemency." To the Tribune he said, "Let it be noted that the Emperor intends to take the lady Pulcheria as his concubine."

"Concubine?" This word had not occurred to the Emperor as a description of Pulcheria.

The Tribune helpfully suggested a synonym: "Bed-mate."

"Your clemency, we presume, wishes to enjoy her," said the Consul,

"Well," the Emperor said, feeling his cheeks growing very warm, "I mean, yes, I suppose..."

"Good. Then she will be brought to your bed tonight."

"What?—No, you—I mean, well, that would be, but, if she, what I—what I mean is, you can't just put her in my bed. She has to want to be there."

"Well, of course she'll want to be there," said the Tribune. "For the Emperor every woman is willing."

"But I mean really want to. You can't just command her."

"Why not?" asked the Tribune, but the Consul quickly interrupted him.

"She is to be delivered willingly. Very good, your clemency."

"Don't you think I should be asking her myself if... if she wants to... to do... that?"

"No," said the Tribune.

"It is not done that way," said the Consul, which the Emperor had to take as true, since he had no notion of how it was done. And the idea of Pulcheria in bed with him was powerfully attractive.

"But she has to be willing," the Emperor repeated. "It

has to be what she wants."

"Of course," the Consul agreed, wearing his working smile.

"And it will be," the Tribune added.

"And one more thing," said the Emperor, since he seemed to be getting his own way. "I don't want any musicians. The orchestra has the night off."

"But there has to be music," the Tribune objected.

But again the Consul interrupted him:

"The Master of the Emperor's Music will be informed."

For the rest of the day the Emperor felt a wonderful and dreadful anticipation. Was Pulcheria really going to be in his bed tonight? He still felt there was something wrong about having someone else suggest the idea. But if she agreed—oh, there were things he was longing to do with her, things he couldn't imagine doing with anyone else. But suppose she refused to come to him: then what? How would he endure the disappointment? And yet why was there something in the back of his mind that said that anything he did with her would also be a disappointment —that even if he did every one of those things he had seen in the mosaic, it could not possibly be enough to satisfy him? How absurdly greedy he must be! He almost despaired as he bathed in the box in the Pool of St. Tryphaena (where Jerome decided to take a swim as well)—but then the thought of Pulcheria's lips against his came back to him, and he thought that surely it would be enough, wouldn't it? But suppose she wouldn't come!— and his mind rolled back around on the wheel of hope and dread.

When at last the night had come, he still lurched from

hope to despair and back again, even as his valets dressed
him in his imperial nightclothes, even when they left a
lampstand to shed a soft light on his bed, even when the
chief of the valets told him, "The lady will be with you
shortly, your clemency." Jerome took his place on a luxu-
riously cool spot between the rugs, and the Emperor sat
on the bed and waited.

Then she appeared. She came in at the dim doorway,
dressed in billowing gauze; and as she moved through the
shadows she seemed almost to be a spirit wafting through
the air. She came gradually into the light, however, and
then it became clear that she was no spirit, nor was she
gauze clean through like the love tutor. She had been
worked over by artists in beauty, but all their efforts had
not been able to suppress her natural charm, hard as they
had tried. The Emperor felt his heart pounding, because
he had never desired anything in his life as much as he
desired Pulcheria, but it was still not certain that he
would have her. The decision could not be his.

She was standing in front of him; he took her hand,
and she sat on the bed beside him.

"Pulcheria," he said almost in a whisper, "I need to
know—I need to ask—is this your choice? Do you want
to be here?"

She smiled at him. "I was told you'd ask that. I was
told my answer ought to be yes."

"No! They can't demand this! I forb——"

She put her finger to his lips.

"And when I heard that," she continued softly, "I
knew the answer *would* be yes. Not because I was compelled, but because you refused to compel me. I didn't
come here for the Emperor. I came here for you. I came

because I do want exactly what you want."

"So you're happy with—with this arrangement?"

"Nothing in the world is perfect," she replied, glancing down at her hand in his. Then she looked back into his eyes. "But this is how I can have your love, and I don't think I want to live without it."

The Emperor tried to think of an answer, and then saw in her eyes that she did not expect an answer in words. By a natural force of attraction their lips came together, and the music swelled upward in a soaring flight of—

Suddenly the Emperor drew back.

"Are there musicians in here?" he demanded in his best imperial voice.

The music stopped. There was a dense silence, and then a timid voice from behind a curtain said, "Um... no."

"Shut up!" said another voice in a raspy whisper.

Pulcheria laughed, "Let them play," she said. "Wasn't that 'The Lost Shepherdess'?"

"I think so," the Emperor replied. To the musicians he said, "You may continue."

The music began again.

"Isn't the rebec a beautiful instrument?" Pulcheria remarked. And then she turned back to her lover, and their lips were drawn together again, and the Emperor found that he had no trouble concentrating on the kiss at all. He found his arms clasping her, and her mouth responding to his in the most thrilling way, and the scent of exotic spices filled his nostrils, and he knew that he was created for this.

When the kiss finally ended, he said quietly, "I—well, I don't quite know everything about, about what to do, you know. I mean, I've seen some mosaics, but I've only had one lesson."

"Don't worry," she said. "I've had the complete course. You could start with this clasp." She placed his hand on the silver clasp on her shoulder. It took him a moment to discover the pin and how to unfasten it, but then the clasp turned out to be a magic key that unlocked all the folds of gauze. From there Pulcheria showed him what to do with his hands and his lips, and he was a perfect student. Everything he had imagined about loving her was true, and a thousand times better than true; and suddenly a dazzling starburst of clarity filled his soul, and he knew what was missing, what was needed, what absolutely *must be* to lift the shadow of disappointment.

"Pulcheria!" he gasped into her ear. "Pulcheria, be my empress! Be my wife!"

She might have refused him; she might have told him it could never be; she might have reminded him that he was the Emperor; but she had reached a state where only one word was left in her vocabulary, and the word was *yes*, and she repeated it over and over.

There was a creaking squawk from the rebec, and the music ground to a halt after a brief but indescribable tangle of dissonances.

Only after he had got his breath back, and Pulcheria was no longer crushing him in her embrace, did the Emperor hear the silence. He had forgotten there was music until he heard the silence. Well, let the musicians be as stunned as they liked. His beautiful, divine Pulcheria would be Empress. The Emperor's word was law. She had fallen beside him, and he held her hand to his lips and kissed it over and over again while she panted and whispered, "I love you."

But suddenly the chief of the valets was in the chamber. "Your clemency!" he announced. "A crisis in the East!"

"What?" The Emperor grasped at whatever bedclothes came to hand and flung them over Pulcheria. "Why are—"

"The Consul sends his most profound apologies, but your clemency's presence is urgently required." The chief of the valets was rather ostentatiously averting his eyes as Pulcheria pulled more of the bedclothes around herself.

"It's the middle of the night!" the Emperor objected. "And we were just— we were—"

"I believe there is disastrous news from the Aspersian front," the chief of the valets explained in a very apologetic tone.

"Oh— Well, I'd better—"

The chief of the valets already had the Emperor's robes ready and got him into them while the Emperor apologized to Pulcheria, who seemed very distressed. "I'm really sorry. Nothing like this has ever— But you meant it, didn't you? You meant it when you said yes?"

"I meant it," she said quietly. "Remember that, whatever happens."

"I'm sure this will be over soon," he said as his sandals were being bound on. "I'll be gone a while, but then—"

He suddenly fell on the bed and kissed her vigorously, and she gripped him and held him as tight as she could.

Then he followed the chief of the valets toward the door.

Jerome, who saw that his friend was going somewhere,

stood up, stretched thoroughly, and padded off after him, Thus he was not there a few minutes later when Pulcheria also left, not entirely under her own power.

CHAPTER 19

A SIMPLE CHOICE

THE news from the East was dire, although privately the Emperor thought it might just possibly have waited until the morning. It seemed there had been a disastrous defeat of some sort, and the Empire's best general had been killed, which meant that a new general had to be appointed. A candidate was presented for the Emperor's approval, which of course was given, and a messenger would be dispatched forthwith to convey the confirmation. No, it would not be advisable for the Emperor to visit the eastern armies himself. Yes, it was true that the Emperor's presence might be inspiring; but, on the other hand, the soldiers' reluctance to expose their Emperor to any risk would encourage a fatal caution that the enemy would be quick to exploit. The best course was to allow the new general to take command and deliver the crushing counterattack of which the imperial army was certainly capable.

All this was explained at inordinate length by the Consul and the Tribune, who seemed occasionally to be confused about the details, probably owing to the late hour and the recent arrival of the report. Eventually, however, the business was as concluded as it could possibly be, and the Emperor felt he could not delay his own news any longer. He dreaded the unpleasant confrontation it would doubtless provoke, but love would give him the iron will he needed.

"I have news of my own," he announced. "The lady Pulcheria has consented to be my wife."

This announcement did not create the consternation he had expected. He did get perhaps the answer he had thought he would get, but not expressed with any real urgency.

"It was expected," said the Consul, "that you would marry the Sultan's daughter."

"It's been arranged," the Tribune added.

"Spring Garden Under the Weather is young," said the Emperor. "She has plenty of time to find another husband."

"This will complicate relations with your most loyal vassal," said the Consul.

"My decision is made."

"Your clemency's will is law, of course," the Consul replied. "When the current emergency is past, we can discuss the details of the diplomacy that will be required."

And that was all! It really was possible to get whatever he wanted just by being imperial enough about it.

What was a little vexing and disappointing was that Pulcheria was not in his bed when he returned to his chamber. The lady had been escorted safely back to her house, he was told by the chief of the valets. It was very late, and it was necessary for his clemency to take his rest, which—the chief of the valets came very close to winking here, although an actual wink was of course out of the question—he was likely to be tempted to forgo if the lady were still present. And the Emperor could see a certain wisdom in that, but he resolved that he would not be compelled to sleep alone when Pulcheria was his Empress. How wonderful it would be to fall asleep with her beside him every night, forever and ever! He gave Jerome a few scratches around the mane and then lay down on the bed, remembering exactly where she had been when he last embraced her and imagining that she was still there. Jerome took his place on the cool spot between the rugs, and soon both Emperor and lion were sleeping peacefully.

Pulcheria was not asleep. She was sitting on a finely carved wooden chair in one of her eight rooms, and four soldiers were there to make sure she stayed. She had indeed been escorted back safely, and now she was exceptionally safe. No one could tell her what she was being kept safe from or for, but then no one really had to tell her.

She had waited for hours in the flickering lamplight when at last there was the sound of the front door opening, and footsteps on the floor of the next room; and then the two guards at the doorway of this room parted to allow the entrance of the Consul, followed by the Tribune.

The Consul looked grim. The Tribune looked ghastly. They both gazed at Pulcheria for a few moments, the Consul as if trying to assess her like some hitherto unknown species of creature, the Tribune as if he had already decided that the hitherto unknown species was loathsome and frightening.

"My lady," the Consul said in greeting, and the Tribune looked even sicker.

Pulcheria said nothing. She was well aware that nothing she said would change the outcome of this interview.

"It seems," the Consul said, "that we have a difficulty. May we sit?"

Pulcheria nodded, and the Consul took one of the light wooden chairs from the side of the room, placed it in front of her, and sat. He looked up at the Tribune, who was still standing, and apparently would have preferred to remain so, but after a few moments gave in and pulled up another chair for himself.

The Consul delayed for some time, apparently considering his words; then he began.

"When we arranged for you to be made available for the Emperor's pleasure, we did not anticipate your filling any other role. The report from the Master of the Emperor's Music, therefore, caused us grave concern. His report, furthermore, was confirmed by his clemency himself, who has told us in so many words that you have agreed to be his wife."

"Which is absurd," the Tribune added, but the Consul raised his finger.

"Now, this would present less of a difficulty if we were worshipers of Apollyon, among whom the men take as many wives as they please. In our faith, however, a man takes one wife. An Emperor may, of course, surround himself with concubines if he likes, and in that capacity you would have been no impediment at all to any of our plans. You were meant, my lady, to be a plaything. You were not meant to be an Empress. Surely you knew that."

"I did," she said quietly. "And I might have told him that, only— only I wasn't thinking. I couldn't think."

"We understand," the Consul said. At this point a syllable erupted from the Tribune, but the Consul's finger was enough to suppress the rest. "We understand," he repeated, "and in a sense you can hardly be blamed. You were in the throes of passion, and the wrong answer came out."

"No!"

Both the Consul and the Tribune jerked slightly backward, as if she had slapped them with the word.

"I was in the throes of passion, and the *right* answer came out. I could never have said it otherwise, but it was what I meant."

This reply was enough to stun even the Consul into silence for a moment. The Tribune took advantage of the silence to grumble "I told you it would be a disaster" without interference from the upraised index finger.

"My lady," the Consul said at last, "you do understand that—"

"Yes, I do understand. I've known your Emperor for a week, and I already know him better than you do, because I know that he's a man. You treat him like a statue, but he's not. He's a good and decent man, and nobody loves him. All he wants is love! I couldn't help loving him, and still I would have told him no, but I think it would have killed me."

"Saying yes might have killed all of us," the Tribune said angrily.

The Consul raised his finger, and there was silence. He looked at Pulcheria, and then past her, and then at her again. "Unfortunately," he said at last, "the Tribune is correct. The betrothal is not...tenable."

"I gave him my word," Pulcheria said quietly.

"That indeed is our difficulty," said the Consul.

"How can I go back on my word?" Now tears were beginning to roll down her cheeks.

"I do not believe he would accept it if you did," said the Consul. "He would suspect us of interfering. He would beg and plead with you until you told him why you were refusing him. Heaven only knows what else he might drag out of you."

Pulcheria was silent, somehow shedding copious tears without actually weeping in any other obvious way, as if she were a miraculous image whose eyes poured forth tears while her face remained serene.

"No," the Consul continued, "as of now it is your continued existence that can no longer be sustained."

She did not flinch, but she gave the Consul a look of such pure contempt that he felt compelled to justify his statement.

"Two thousand people, my lady—two thousand at the least—depend on things remaining as they are. Two thousand good and decent people in this palace—"

"No," she said. "Two thousand people, but there's only one good and decent one."

"As you wish," said the Consul. "His life is as bound up with the state of things as the rest of ours—infinitely more so, in fact."

"He doesn't have a life. You won't let him have one. And I make him happy! I don't know why or how, but I can feel it! Doesn't he deserve to be happy?"

"He is not required to be happy. He is required to be Emperor." The Consul leaned back a little. "The difficulty, in fact, is that he has conceived some mistaken notion of personal happiness, which for reasons we cannot fathom he associates with you. As long as you continue to exist, you will be an insuperable obstacle. It is unfortunate for you, of course, but decisions must often be made for the greater good that have unfortunate effects on certain individuals. I believe you understand the necessity of this decision as well as we do."

Pulcheria opened her mouth, but for some time no words came out. The Consul waited patiently. At last she was able to articulate a question: "What are you going to do with me?"

"We came here to discuss exactly that," said the Consul, "It could, of course, be considered presumptuous in the highest degree for you to have attempted to make yourself Empress. And you are familiar with the prescribed penalty for presumption."

She was, but her face maintained its tearful impassivity.

"But," the Consul continued, "it may not be necessary to bring out the cauldron in order to terminate this regrettable business successfully, Neither the Tribune nor I have any desire for excessive cruelty." The Tribune made a face suggesting that, in this particular case, excessive cruelty might be exactly to his taste; but he said nothing, and the Consul continued. "Under the circumstances, your continued existence in our Emperor's world can of course no longer be sustained. The means of your exit, however, are open to...adjustment. It can be lingering and unpleasant, as you know. But perhaps alternate arrangements can be made."

At this Pulcheria finally lost her battle for composure. But she was able to bring out a few wavering words before she dissolved in sobs:

"Will he know that I loved him?"

The Consul appeared to be genuinely affected. "I will see to it," he said.

CHAPTER 20

A TRAGIC DEMISE

IT WAS a hot day of alternating clouds and sun, the clouds big and fluffy, forming all kinds of extravagant sculptures as they ambled across the sky. Seen from the Stoa, the city across the Narrows was less distinct than usual, its domes and minarets paler and bluer. Iamblichus, who made no remark about the lion (depriving the Emperor of his opportunity to repeat the joke about the lion hunt). explained that the effect was due to a thickening of the ether caused by heat. But that was not the subject of the lesson this morning. The subject was death.

"All men are mortal," Iamblichus was saying, "and death is the end of all life. By 'end' I mean both senses of the word: for death is the cessation of life, but it is also the purpose of life."

It took the Emperor a few moments to react to that statement, because most of his mind was dedicated to meditating on that moment of explosive revelation when Pulcheria had said yes. But when Iamblichus' words penetrated to the core of his conscious mind, the Emperor was not entirely ready to accept them.

"I thought the purpose of life was...being good or

something. Or love. Why isn't love the purpose of life?"

"It is another way of saying the same thing."

"What do you mean? How is 'love is the purpose of life' the same as 'death is the purpose of life'?"

"Consider what we know about life. That the soul is immortal is easily demonstrated: indeed, it may be the only easily demonstrated fact of philosophy. In previous lessons we have learned the six proofs of the immortality of the soul, which we may review later if your clemency requests it. For the moment, however, let us take the immortality of the soul as granted. The brevity of human life in this world is too well known to require comment: you have but to search your own memory to discover how rare it is for a man to live even a paltry century. To that observation add the fact of the immortality of the soul, and it must become obvious that this life is but a preparation for the next. If, therefore, death is in fact our birth into that next life, then we can truly say that the purpose of this life is to prepare us for that next life. Thus the purpose of life is death, which is to say our entry into the next life. Now, what more efficaciously—"

The Emperor was drifting away from Iamblichus by this point. His mind had run back to Pulcheria—Pulcheria's voice, Pulcheria's laugh, Pulcheria's eyes. Oh, how he loved her immortal soul—but, oh, how delightful it was that the soul was wrapped in such luscious flesh! This must be why faith promised the resurrection of the body. After his evening with Pulcheria he was sure he knew what heaven must be like.

"Doesn't our religion teach the resurrection of the body?" he asked suddenly, interrupting whatever Iamblichus had been saying, which was not as interesting as bodies, specifically Pulcheria's.

"Well, yes," Iamblichus conceded. His tone made it clear that this was a concession. "The dogmas of revelation are, of course, not subject to philosophical investigation, but—"

"Why not?"

"They just aren't," Iamblichus replied a bit shortly. Then he resumed his accustomed patience. "The principles of religion are *revealed*; the principles of philosophy are *discovered*. They are two entirely different fields of study, though they do tend in the same direction. In this case, for example, philosophy and religion concur in the fact of human immortality. They agree that death is not to be feared but welcomed."

"But if I lunged at you with a sword, I'll bet you'd jump out of the way."

Iamblichus smiled his most indulgent smile. "Perhaps I am an imperfect philosopher."

After that cane a session with Sozomen. Jerome liked Sozomen right away for some reason: he had been indifferent to Iamblichus, who for his part had been indifferent to the lion; but with Sozomen, who was terrified, Jerome was very affectionate. It was clearly some effort for the history tutor to concentrate on the already difficult task of determining whether Adrianus XIX belonged among the Good Emperors or the Wicked Emperors. Every time Sozomen returned to the subject, the lion rubbed his head against the poor man's knees. In the end, Sozomen decided that Number Nineteen was a Good Emperor, in spite of his many flaws, and ignoring his military accomplishments, because he had crushed an outbreak of the Nicolaitan heresy.

"What about me?" asked the current Emperor.

"What about...what?" asked Sozomen, adding "My goodness" under his breath as Jerome attempted to present his head for scratching.

"Am I a Good Emperor or a Wicked Emperor?"

"Your clemency is a Good Emperor, of course," Sozomen replied.

"Why?"

"Heavens," said Sozomen: Jerome's whole head was on in his lap. "Oh,—why? Because the reigning Emperor is Good by definition."

"Oh." This was a disappointing answer.

"Is this lion likely to be with us in future lessons?" Sozomen asked in a desperately conversational tone.

"Scratch his head," the Emperor suggested. "He likes that. Especially behind the ears."

Sozomen forced a sickly smile and very slowly placed a pair of fingers on the lion's head. When the fingers started to move, Jerome responded to the feeble scratching with an expression of serene contentment. Sozomen still looked terrified.

The clouds were bigger, less fluffy and more mountainous, by the time Sozomen's lesson was over. The Consul and the Tribune reappeared soon after, but the Emperor surprised himself by successfully demanding a walk alone on the Great Colonnade. All he had to do was insist, and "It will be our pleasure to accompany you" turned into "As your clemency wishes, of course." So for the first time he could remember the Emperor found himself strolling along the promenade between the columns unaccompanied.

The Great Colonnade was deserted. He realized almost with a start that it was deserted because of him: that there were times when he had seen senators and their families from his window as they strolled along the promenade, but that they were always evicted for the sake of the Emperor. Perhaps some day he would be imperial enough to command that they be allowed to stay, and he and Pulcheria could stroll among them, almost like real people.

He stopped and looked out over the water for a while. The clouds had blocked the sun now, and in the southwest they were dark. A storm was coming in. Perhaps he would stay out and watch the storm. Perhaps he would even get a little wet if the wind blew the rain under the roof. It might be a delightful thing to be rained on. Would that be allowed?

The sea led to everywhere, and he still wondered what everywhere was like. But he found himself thinking that everywhere had lost some of its attraction. Here was as good as anywhere. It might be amusing to go somewhere else in the world with Pulcheria sometime, but "with Pulcheria" was the important thing.

The dark clouds were closer now, and the Emperor could see a sheet of rain dragging across the water toward the end of the Colonnade. He thought he ought to get in out of the rain, and then he thought again that perhaps he ought to let it rain on him, and then he wondered how Jerome would react to being rained on. He looked down at Jerome, who simply accepted the world as it came to him and found most of it delightful (except, of course, for the Consul, whom the lion continued to regard with deep suspicion). Jerome would probably be delighted by rain.

A few fat drops had begun to fall in the water and on

the roof now, and the wind was picking up and driving some of the drops into the Emperor's face, which was pleasant only because no one was telling him it must not happen. Jerome was sitting, his eyes flicking shut when drops came at him, but otherwise showing no signs of annoyance. The imperial valets would supply the Emperor with dry clothes: why shouldn't he stand out here and watch the storm? There was a flash of lightning out over the water, and a few moments later a rumble of thunder, and for that reason the Emperor did not hear the voice behind him the first time it spoke.

"Your clemency," the voice repeated.

Startled, the Emperor turned to find a young man holding out a rolled-up document—a letter or something.

"A message, your clemency," the young man said timidly.

"Oh—thank you," said the Emperor, taking the scroll. The young man made the proper obeisance and walked away toward the passage through to the walk that led up to the forum. The Emperor, meanwhile, unrolled the document, which did prove to be a letter:

> The lady Pulcheria to her most beloved Emperor, greetings.
>
> My love, I have seen on sober reflection the impossibility of our union, and I understand how disastrous it must prove for our Empire. And yet so sincere was I in my protestations of love that I am certain I could not have lived without you. I beg you not to take my death—

"Stop!" the Emperor cried out to the messenger. He began to run toward the young man. A hole had been kicked in his stomach; he was forgetting to breathe, and he had to suck in a chestful of air to speak when he caught up. "Who gave this to you?" he demanded. "Who?"

"It came from a lady," the messenger told him.

Then he must run to her. If she was thinking—

At this point the Tribune appeared, looking a little out of breath. "Your clemency," he said, "there's been a—a dreadful tragedy—"

"Where?" the Emperor shouted over a nearer clap of thunder. "Who?"

"The Tower of Diotrephes—the lady Pulcheria—"

The Emperor was already running up the walk in what was now pouring rain, with Jerome bounding beside him. If he could just run fast enough—if he could run faster than time—— He stuffed the note into his robe as the rain fell harder.

He was in the Forum now, where some of the vendors were still covering their stalls, and the crowds had dispersed to the porches of the grand buildings round about to wait out the storm; and then up the Via Media that led north out of the Forum through the middle of the palace grounds, Jerome still following. His chest was on fire from the exertion, but he still felt he might somehow outrun the moments——

And then, as the way curved up the Eminence, he saw it.

The cloudburst was coming to an end. A few people were standing at the base of the Eminence, looking up, occasionally moving forward a little, but always falling back again, as if they did not dare set foot on holy ground. And up on the top of the Eminence, at the base of the tower, was a sprawled figure, dressed in a lady's robes. Beside her the Archeparch was kneeling, and there was no question who the lady was: with a kind of cruel humor the clouds passed away from the sun at that moment, and bright sunlight fell on the tableau, and there was no mistaking the lady's shoulders.

The Emperor had stopped, but now he ran again, until someone in the little arc of people at the base of the Eminence reached out and physically barred his way.

"No, your clemency." It was the Consul. "You mustn't—"

Jerome roared. Jerome was not happy at all that the Consul was attacking his friend, and he pushed between them. But other hands restrained the Emperor as well.

"Let me go!" he shouted.

"Nothing can be done," the Consul said. "The Archeparch gave her the last rites, and—"

"What did you do to her?" the Emperor cried.

And then the will dribbled out of him. There was nothing left. The world had crushed him, and he could not stand under its weight. He fell back from the restraining arms, turned, and started to walk away.

"Your clemency—" the Consul began.

"Don't follow me," the Emperor said, just loud enough to be heard.

He walked away, toward the Forest of Arches, and only Jerome dared to follow. It was a strange emptiness that carried him forward. The world had ended, and this was what it was like to live past the end. He ought to have been wailing like a tragedian. He ought to have been calling on heaven to annihilate him. But instead he was walking into the Forest of Arches, silent and quite

aware of the sights and scents and sounds around him,
The sunlight was terribly and unnaturally bright against
the dark clouds still rolling through the sky, especially in
the east. Raindrops sparkled on leaves, and the smell of
mignonette weighed down the humid air. Thunder spoke
occasionally, but not in anger, only as if it were mumbling
to itself in the distance. The rain had made patterns on
the old stones; some of them turned darker when they
were wet, and some did not, and part of the Emperor
wondered why that was, and another part was very angry
with him for thinking such thoughts when we ought to be
wallowing in grief and despair. His wet robe clung to him
as he walked, and he felt the weight of it, which in the
abstract was an interesting sensation; for the first time he
really thought about what it meant to be wet, and realized that a robe that was wet was actually carrying water
somehow, and it would be interesting to know how that
was accomplished, and whether the fabric was full of in-
finitesimal vessels in which the water was deposited. And
he was furious with himself for not being able to feel the
grief, not giving way to a torrent of tears, not feeling anything but a heightened awareness of his bodily senses:
the sparkle of the raindrops, the more and more distant
mumbling of the storm, the scent of wet lion, the weight
and chill of his dripping robes. And when at last he
reached the little chamber with the ancient altar (he had
not really realized he was heading there, but of course he
ended up there), he sat on the stone and looked at the
sparkles of the raindrops on the toadflax, red and yellow
and aquamarine sparkles, and thought how every precious
bead of water, if you looked at it close enough, contained
the whole world turned upside down, a world that would

fall and shatter in a while, but not right now.

Meanwhile Jerome joined him on the stone and lay down with his head on the Emperor's lap, and the Emperor scratched behind the lion's damp ears, and the two of them stayed there most of the afternoon, surrounded by the filthy mocking beauty of the material world.

CHAPTER 21

THE NECESSARY ARRANGEMENTS

THE Emperor woke with early sunlight streaming obliquely into his chamber, and there was a moment of blissful ordinariness before the weight of the previous day fell on him and he remembered,

He had slept very well. He had got rid of the imperial bedchamber orchestra with threats of physical violence, and in the silence and emptiness, with only the gentle sea outside his window to lull him to sleep with its lazy waves, sleep had descended almost at once. Now he felt guilty about that, too. It ought not to have been easy to sleep: he ought to have lain awake all night, or if he had slept he ought to have been tormented by nightmares. Instead, he had slept as peacefully as if the world had not ended yesterday. And where were the floods of tears? There were supposed to be floods of tears, not the quiet void that only anger could fill.

The morning tonic arrived at the appointed time. The Emperor took the little glass and examined it for a length of time that worried his valets. "Your clemency's morning tonic," the chief of the valets said eventually. At that the Emperor turned, strode over to his window, and dumped the tonic on the promenade below.

Then he came back and, while the valets were still gaping in mute horror, took the peach from the little tray and bit into it. But the sweetness was more galling than the tonic would have been, and he found that he couldn't finish the whole thing. He left the remains on the tray and allowed the valets to dress him in his day robes. More things were brought for him to eat, but the very notion of eating seemed absurd to him, and he wondered how he could ever have brought himself to perform the operation. He gave the whole lot to Jerome, who left the sunny spot he had found near the window and examined the offerings, selecting some of them as suitable for lions and leaving the rest to go off and visit his sand-pit.

Then it was time, so he was told, for an audience. He was brought to the vestry behind the Hall of Lions: he must have walked on his own feet, since he had no memory of being carried; but his hyperawareness of the afternoon before had given way to dull indifference, and his mind had begun to dwell on what might have been different if—— if anything had been different.

Jerome stuck with him even more closely than he had done in the past few days, as if he sensed that some deep sickness of the heart was afflicting his friend, for which the only possible cure was continuous affection from a well-disposed lion.

The purple robe of Adrianus XII was as itchy as ever, but the Emperor felt as if he deserved the itch and hardly made any adjustments to the thing at all. Then he sat on the throne and watched the Consul and the Tribune make the long march down the hall toward him, which was pointless and absurd. Jerome roared reliably when the Consul came near, and so the audience officially began. The Consul and the Tribune were staring at him expectantly, but what they expected the Emperor could hardly guess.

"The greeting, your clemency," the Consul said quietly.

"Oh. The greeting. The Emperor's condiments to the People and Senate."

There was a brief pause as the Consul and the Tribune considered what to do about this slightly garbled greeting. The main thing was that it had reversed the proper order of Senate and People, and what did that mean for their traditional replies? After a few moments, the Tribune responded to some slight nods and gestures from the Consul and gave his reply first.

"The greetings of the people to the Emperor, the guardian of their rights."

Then the Consul, looking resigned, added, "The greetings of the Senate to the Emperor, the bearer of their burdens."

Then there was silence again.

At last the Consul spoke, since the Emperor clearly had no intention of speaking first. "To begin with, the Senate and People would like to express their most sincere condolences. The tragedy of yesterday has affected all of us deeply. The necessary arrangements have been made, and the—"

"What arrangements?" the Emperor demanded.

"The funeral and burial, your clemency." He spoke in a muted and apologetic tone, as if he had hoped to avoid mentioning those distasteful terms.

"Oh." The Emperor had never thought about funerals

and how they came to be. He had been to funerals, of course: it was customary for the Emperor to attend the funerals of senators, and he had a sharp and strongly colored memory from when he was nine years old of the funeral of the old Archeparch, a spectacle that had wrapped the idea of death in a majesty that he had found pleasant to contemplate when he was young. But he had never thought at all about what made funerals happen. It had always seemed as though the death caused the funeral to occur by natural and inevitable processes. But of course someone must have made arrangements.

"What kinds of arrangements have been made?" he asked, interrupting the Consul, who had been saying something about something.

"Well, a quiet, private funeral, and a place in the senatorial burying-ground—"

"She was an Empress," the Emperor declared, sitting up in his throne. He had not realized how much he had slumped. "She will have a funeral befitting an Empress."

This statement provoked a conspicuous intake of breach in both the Consul and the Tribune, followed by an exchange of glances, followed by a bit of rumbling and clicking as the Consul attempted to formulate his next utterance. "The, the—— technically, that is, she is, she belonged to, —what I mean, of course, is that, as she had not yet been joined in matrimony to, to you—"

"She was my Empress," the Emperor said, "The ceremony had not taken place, but the— the sacramental union had." The argument was coming to him surprisingly easily: he must have paid some attention when the Archeparch had tried to teach him some theology a few years before. "If there can be baptism by desire, then

there can be marriage by desire, when the consummation
has taken place but there has not been time to perform
the ceremony before... before..."

It was odd: he found himself unable to speak the word.
There was one word missing from his sentence, and he
simply could not produce it.

The Consul, from long habit in dealing with these little
difficulties, put on his working smile, which might perhaps have been a little out of place in such a discussion as
this. "The other difficulty, or perhaps I should simply say
the other matter, is the question of suicide. Considering
the mental state involved, the Archeparch has been willing to be, as one night say, broad-minded, and—"

"The Emperor's will is law!" the Emperor shouted. In
fact it came out as more of a broken screech, because the
Emperor had very little practice in shouting. But Jerome
added a roar to show that he concurred, and the effect on
the whole was impressive enough to put an end to all de-
bate.

"As your clemency wishes, of course," the Consul said
quietly. Without having obviously taken any steps, he
was now standing some distance further back from the
imperial dais than he had been before the lion had
roared.

"What else?" the Emperor asked wearily. He felt as if
he ought to apologize for his outburst, but he could not
bring himself to do it.

"There is an entry from the Potters' Guild for your
clemency's judgment."

"Not today," said the Emperor, which was so unexpected and uncharacteristic that at first neither the Consul nor the Tribune heard the words correctly. The Em-

peror stood up. "I'm through with the audience for now. Have the Archeparch deal with the funeral arrangements. I'm going back to my chamber." He stepped down from the dais and headed toward the vestry, leaving the Consul and the Tribune, mute and inert, gaping after him. Jerome followed, of course, and the two of them walked unaccompanied—an odd sensation for the Emperor—along the narrow corridor that led from the vestry around the Hall of Lions to the grand passageway. The Emperor felt guilty about terminating the audience so abruptly, and he added that to the big pile of things he probably ought to apologize for later when he felt up to it. Right now there was a task awaiting him, and although he could not imagine how he would have the courage to do it, it would have to be done sooner or later.

The imperial bedchamber was flooded with light, because it was the time of the morning when the sun was still low enough to send its rays under the roof of the Great Colonnade and straight into the big southeast-facing window. The Emperor seldom saw the chamber at this time of day: he was usually out somewhere doing something imperial. It was a cheerful place when it was bright like this, and the cheerfulness was insulting. But the light would make it that much easier to do the thing he dreaded doing.

The long walk across the floor to the great imperial bed was not nearly long enough. He reached the bed too soon. It was already carefully made up, but from long experience he knew that it would be four more days until the pillows were changed, and that was where he had put the letter: in the cover of one of the pillows. He did not in general have personal possessions: since everything be-

longed to him, nothing belonged to him. Now that he had
one thing that was actually precious for its own sake, he
had to find ways of keeping it safe from the ordinary daily
maintenance of the imperial household.

Safe though it was, however, he had not yet read it all
the way through. He owed it to the Empress—he had
started to call her that in his own mind—to read her last
words. But he had not been able to do it yet.

Jerome, seeing his friend sitting on the bed with a pil-
low in his lap and no signs of activity, fell over and
stretched on the floor, waiting for somebody to remember the lion. He yawned after a while, because there was
nothing better to do.

At last the Emperor found the strength to retrieve the
letter from the pillow-cover. The papyrus had warped
with the dampness of the rain, but the black ink on it had
not run: it looked like the thick black ink that was always
used on the official documents that were brought to him
to sign in his own imperial purple. He read the greeting
and stopped at the words "most beloved Emperor" and
remembered her in that very bed telling him she loved
him, that she couldn't live without his love. And she had
it! Why couldn't she believe that? But she did, didn't
she? That was the reason. She knew that he would have
her as his Empress come what might, and she was afraid
for the Empire. That was probably what the rest of the
letter said. But it was impossible to read, He had tried
once already, and he had gone as far as "I beg you not to
take my death…"—and that word had kicked the breath
out of him again, just as it had done in the Great Colonnade: again that sudden bolt of fear struck his heart, and
it seemed as if he ought to be running toward or away

from something.

No, it was not possible to read the rest of it yet. Soon. The Emperor stuffed the letter into his robe and sat on the bed until someone came and took him to dinner, Most of his dinner went into Jerome. After that he waited for darkness and went to bed. This time there seemed to be no question of sleeping, so he allowed the orchestra to play, because he could think about the music instead of thinking of the things he would say to Pulcheria if he could. And really the only thing he thought of to say was a question, but he thought it over and over: If you loved me, why did you hate me so much?

The funeral happened two days later. It was magnificently somber, with a casket befitting an Empress (closed, of course, because of the unfortunate damage which the Consul was sure he did not have to describe) and pomp and ceremony as impressive as the Emperor remembered from the funeral of the old Archeparch twelve and a half years before. Everyone who could fit into the Church of the Assumption attended. A carefully redacted version of the Emperor's tragic love story having been prepared and whispered to the whispering classes, who would be sure to spread it efficiently, everyone was watching the Emperor, and everyone praised the young Emperor's dignity and composure. But it was only emptiness. His eyes were dry because he had no tears to shed. He was sure that there was something wrong with him.

CHAPTER 22

A DISTRACTION

THE Emperor was mostly inert the next day, and the day after that. He spent some time sitting on the Stoa and some time walking through the Forest of Arches. Most of the day he slept. Jerome approved wholeheartedly of the sleeping and joined in it enthusiastically. At night the orchestra played until the Emperor felt pity for the musicians and feigned sleep so that they could stop playing.

The Consul and the Tribune were worried. The Consul mentioned his worry after the Emperor failed to appear at all for his morning audience, sending word through the chief of his valets (who looked miserable delivering the message and had to be reassured that he was not to blame) that he would rather not have an audience today, and would probably spend the morning sleeping.

"It is troubling," the Consul said once he was alone with the Tribune.

"I told you it would be a disaster," the Tribune remarked. It was far from the first time he had made that remark, and he would probably make it again.

"I am not sure whether we require so strong a term as 'disaster,'" said the Consul. "But it is clear that, in the next few days or weeks, our Emperor will require careful management. His mind is dwelling in an unhealthy manner on his perceived loss, which, with the natural tendency of youth to exaggerated passions, he has magnified into an epic tragedy. He feels obliged to manifest outward signs of grief."

"But the Master of the Emperor's Music says he never weeps in the night. Aren't you supposed to weep in the night?"

"Precisely, my dear Tribune. The grief is a performance, which he feels obliged to put on for our benefit. The longer he indulges it, the more natural it will become, and the more he will become accustomed to shirking his imperial duties. What we need is something to distract him—something to bring simple joy back into his life."

"Should we try a harlot again? I mean, now that we've got rid of the floor-scrubber."

"I don't think that would have the proper effect. No, I was thinking of some sort of public entertainment, the sort of thing he has always enjoyed in the past."

"Oh!" said the Tribune, as if seized by sudden inspiration, "What was that play he liked so much last year?"

"You mean the Tragedy of Diotrephes?"

"Yes! That was it! We could have the... have... oh, yes, I can see the problem with that."

The Consul nodded. And then, after a few moments' thought, he said, "Nevertheless, you and I are thinking in a similar manner. Perhaps something in the theater—not a play, but a spectacle: something with color and diversion enough to make our Emperor think of other things than the grief he has taken upon himself."

The Tribune nodded with half-lidded eyes to indicate sage wisdom. "But how will we make him agree to the thing?"

"We shall have to give that our most thorough consideration," said the Consul.

The Emperor, meanwhile, did sleep much of that morning. He slept because he had not slept much during the night. He had discovered his own guilt, and it was a thing worth dwelling on. He had taken her—the feminine personal pronoun had only one referent in his mind—to the Eminence; he had told her the story of Diotrephes, with its tragic ending that she had imitated; he had taken her inside the tower, where she could see the ascent to the top. Would she have leapt from the tower if he had not shown her the way—if he had not taken her there and said, "This is what you do if you're disappointed in love"? No, he had been responsible: he had killed her as surely as if he had pushed her from the top of the tower himself. And it was good to have a reason to blame himself. He had been trying to blame himself for some time now, but he had not found a good way to place the blame. Now he had it worked out.

It was a little after noon when the Emperor finally sat up and decided to get out of bed. He bound on his sandals and walked out of his chamber without anyone's noticing, as far as he could tell. Then he went around the corner and out into the open air of the Great Colonnade.

Here he simply stool for a while, with Jerome sitting beside him, and looked out over the sea, He was not looking at anything in particular, although there were colorful sails to see and it was a particularly fine and clear day to see them. He did wonder for a while how one went about getting properly drowned; but although the idea of not existing any longer did appeal to him, he understood that it could not be, because no one else would take care of Jerome properly. It was odd that he cared nothing for the whole vast Empire that supposedly depended on him, but he would continue to exist for the lion's sake. There must be something wrong with him.

A rumbling was coming from Jerome. The Emperor looked down at his lion, and then followed Jerome's eyes to see the Consul standing at a respectful distance on the promenade (Jerome inspired respect in the Consul), with the Tribune behind him.

"Please pardon our intrusion, your clemency," the Consul said, "but if you can spare a moment to discuss a—"

The Tribune sneezed, and half a dozen sparrows suddenly took off from the capital of the column beside him.

The Consul continued: "—to discuss a tribute to the late Empress..."

The Emperor had been ready to say that he could not presently spare a moment because he was busy moping, but hearing the Empress mentioned made him more receptive. "A tribute?"

The Consul nodded. "The mourning period will be over in a few days," he began—

—and the Emperor thought that was an absurd idea, because the mourning period had hardly begun, and would surely last the rest of his life—

"—and it seemed to us that your clemency might wish to impress the memory of the late Empress on the minds of the Senate and People in a favorable manner."

The Emperor thought about this for a while. Like

many of the things the Consul said, it seemed to have a great many more words than thoughts, and yet it hinted obliquely at things that could have been said directly. It probably meant that the Emperor was supposed to supply a few words of response to keep the conversation going. "Favorable? What do you mean?"

The Tribune sneezed again, but he had exhausted the nearby sparrows with his first sneeze. The Consul was about to resume, but the Tribune decided to sneeze again. After waiting a moment to see whether a third sneeze was forthcoming, the Consul continued:

"We had thought, perhaps, that a spectacle in honor of the late Empress might both divert the people after a time of grief and inspire sentiments of gratitude toward the Empress in whose name it was given. Such entertainments have often been presented by past Emperors in honor of their predecessors, and invariably with success."

The Tribune sneezed, which interrupted what the Consul had intended to say; but he had already made an attractive presentation.

"I think it might be good," the Emperor said. "Have it done." He began to turn back to face the sea again.

"We had thought," the Consul said quickly, "that your clemency might wish to supervise the preparations. In honor of the late Empress."

The Emperor stopped and gave this proposal several moments of serious consideration.

"No," he said at last. "I don't think that will be necessary. I trust you to deal with it." He turned to face the sea.

That was the last the Emperor saw of the Consul and the Tribune that day. In the late afternoon he took

Jerome for a walk in the Forest of Arches, where the lion enjoyed the thyme and the opportunities to leap from one section of low ruined wall to another. In the late evening the Emperor went to bed and listened to the music for quite a long time.

It took the better part of two weeks for the proper arrangements to be made. Fortunately a spectacle had already been in preparation: the schedule was moved forward, the preparations were rushed, and a dancing horse was procured to replace the tame lion. The Emperor could not be prevailed upon, however, to take an interest in these preparations. The best the Consul could get out of him was a promise that he would certainly preside from the imperial box when the spectacle was presented: that, yes, he could undertake to do, but he was feeling a little off, and would probably not be up to formal audiences before then.

The Emperor spent much of that time developing intricate variations on his new theory of guilt. He walked up and down in the Great Colonnade and took Jerome for long walks in the Forest of Arches. Wherever he went, he could see the Tower of Diotrephes up there on its hill. It was there to remind him of his guilt: that had become its only purpose. No invaders came by land or sea, and no sentry was stationed at the top of the tower, but still it stood erect to remind him that she would still be alive if he hadn't loved her. It was not just taking her to the tower that had killed her: it was taking her there because he wanted her for himself. He had no right to that kind of love.

And every once in a while he brought out the letter and tried to read her last words. But each time he got as

far as "I beg you not to take my death"—and stopped.
He could not read past that word. He carried the letter
with him everywhere, but so far it remained unread.

"We must place all our hope in the spectacle," the
Consul told the Tribune. "I have faith that it will make a
profound change in the situation."

When at last the day of the spectacle did come, it was
clear that, as far as attendance was concerned, it was a
great success. Every inhabitant of the palace precinct was
there, more than two thousand people filling the semicir-
cular theater that sat on the south shore of the Pool of St.
Tryphaena. They were all waiting for the appearance of
the Emperor and Jerome—by now everyone had heard of
Jerome, who was as eagerly awaited as the Emperor himself—and when they did appear they were greeted with
enthusiastic cheers. The Emperor and Jerome both received the ovation with great dignity. Jerome was wearing his collar and chain to prevent him from any excessive
enthusiasm, especially since other animals would be per-
forming; but the precaution was probably unnecessary,
since Jerome, whose meat had always come to him without his having to work for it, had no taste for hunting.

The show itself consisted of a series of spectacles with
no other purpose than to amaze and amuse the spectators.
First came a pair of elephants. It was not really necessary
for them to do anything to amaze and delight the audience: it was only necessary for them to be elephants. Nevertheless they performed some simple tricks, ending by
facing each other, standing on their hind legs, and twisting their trunks together, which earned them a big cheer,
and some polite applause from the Emperor himself.

After the elephants came a dozen acrobats, who performed remarkable feats of leaping through the air and landing on one another's shoulders. This performance also pleased the audience, and again gained dutiful acknowledgment from the Emperor. The same was true of the lyre-player who followed, singing one of the ancient panegyrics to Adrianus III or VII or somebody.

The Emperor had come because it was his duty to come, but now he was beginning to forget that he was supposed to be grief-stricken. The amusements were beginning to amuse him. The Consul and the Tribune (they had checked the breeze and, for the convenience of the Tribune, had carefully installed themselves some distance upwind from the lion) nudged each other and exchanged knowing glances. When the troupe of clowns all fell down at once and the Emperor actually let a laugh escape, the Tribune nudged the Consul so hard that the Consul had to suppress a yelp of pain.

And then came the dancing horse. He was called Bucephalus, and he was an animal of remarkable skill. With his master, Bucephalus walked up on the stage with regal dignity. A small orchestra began a stately dance tune, one the Emperor remembered having heard at the masked ball two or three weeks ago. And the horse danced! He followed exactly the steps the Emperor himself had laboriously learned for that rhythm; except that he did it with four legs instead of two, as if he were two dancers. The Emperor was smiling. How he would love to tell her about this! The horse never missed a step. There was a smile on the Emperor's face and a tear rolling down his cheek. And when the music came to an end, the Emperor stood and clapped, and the horse stood right in front of him on the stage and bowed to him. It was wonderfully dignified, and very funny at the same time. It would have delighted her just to hear about it! Without any warning, all the fountains of the great deep were broken up, and the windows of heaven were opened, and all the tears that had waited so long behind the gates came at once. There was only one person in the world who had ever shared joy with him, and she was gone! He started to choke with sobs. Hummingbirds, flowers, lions, sunsets—they meant something because she loved then! Now——Now the whole palace was pressing in on him, he couldn't breathe, he would suffocate, he had to get away from everything in the world. He suddenly turned and, almost blind with stinging tears, stumbled out of the box and began to dash away, toward the right, not going anywhere but away. Jerome followed, dragging his chain behind him; and there was a clear path before them, because no one would stand in the way of an Emperor with a lion.

CHAPTER 23

A DREADFUL SUSPICION

NOTHING like this tempest of grief had ever come over him before, at least not since he had been very young. By the time he was away from the theater, the Emperor was running, as if he could outrun his tears and leave his choking, wracking sobs behind him. Jerome trotted and bounded after him, his chain scraping and clanking along the ground. Together they ran into the Terrace Garden and up some steps and through some shrubbery and onto a path—and there, right beside them, was that trumpet-vine where she had seen the hummingbird. There was where the Emperor gave up: he let himself sink to the ground, and for a while he just sat and wailed like a child, while Jerome, disturbed by his friend's apparent distress, nuzzled him and then sat beside him, almost in his lap. This caused an even stronger convulsion of grief, as the Emperor remembered Jerome nuzzling Pulcheria and how the lion had delighted her. He held Jerome by the neck and wailed and sobbed until he started to cough, and it was some time before he lapsed into silent spasms, burying his face in the patient lion's mane.

The show went on without him. The audience had, in

general, worried about the Emperor's sudden departure; but an announcement that the Emperor had been called away by a sudden emergency sufficed to let them know that it was not advisable to demonstrate that worry. Besides, the Aspersian sword-dancers were next, and they were really quite good.

The Consul and the Tribune, after a brief period of indecision, had gone out to look for the Emperor. They had taken four strong guards with them, because, while one certainly did not expect the Emperor to do anything foolish, no of course not, still it might be wise to have the means of preventing foolishness if foolishness should occur.

"I told you it would be a disaster," the Tribune remarked as he and the Consul walked into the Terrace Garden, following the direction in which the Emperor had last been seen walking. The Consul accepted the observation without remark; it would doubtless be repeated soon, so there would be other opportunities to formulate a reply.

The problem with the Terrace Garden was that it was large and picturesque—ordinarily virtues in an ornamental garden, but virtues that made it hard to find a man who did not necessarily wish to be found. The main paths followed the lines of the terraces, but there were many stairways and twisting ascents between the terraces, making the place almost as labyrinthine as the Forest of Arches.

"Our difficulty," said the Consul as they stopped to rest in the shade of a bush that dangled from the terrace above (for the Consul and the Tribune were not young men)—"Our difficulty is that he might have turned in any direction. He might have stopped, or he might have kept going. He has great reserves of endurance."

"You don't think he'll do something…" The Tribune sniffled a bit as he tried to think of the right word. The first word that had come to mind was "stupid," but that was not a word one applied to the Emperor even in one's own private thoughts. At last he came up with a suitable term: "You don't think he'll do anything unfortunate, do you?"

"I have faith that he will not," the Consul replied, "But by works is faith made perfect. Since we appear to have underestimated the strength of his attachment to the floor-scrubber, it would be foolish in the extreme to underestimate the lengths to which his grief might drive him."

"I told you it would be a disaster," the Tribune remarked.

"Yes," said the Consul. "You told me it would be a disaster. I should like to state it clearly, so that it may be recorded once and for all in your memory, that I am aware that you told me it would be a disaster. You told me that when we allowed him to have her, and you have told me that you told me, often and unambiguously, at every opportunity since then. Let it be registered that I concur, and that I acknowledge I made a mistake. We ought never to have allowed him to have her, and I was wrong, and you were right."

The Tribune sniffled some more, and produced a rag from his robe to wipe his nose. "And now," he said half into the rag, "it almost seems as if getting rid of her was an even bigger mistake."

"It was an unfortunate necessity," the Consul said. "If

it could have been dealt with otherwise, I should have been the first to recommend a different course; but it had become necessary that she should cease to exist. It seems cruel, but—"

"It could have been a lot crueler. The cauldr— the cauldron is a— a——"

The Tribune sneezed, an explosion that echoed from the terraces and was answered by a roar from above.

The two men looked up at once. On the terrace above them Jerome was standing, and beside him the Emperor, and they were both looking down at the two men below them.

Immediately the Consul put on his working smile. "Your clemency! We are gratified to find you here. Of course we did not in the least mistrust your clemency's judgment, but when you left in a state of...of obvious distress, we... we thought we ought to... Accidents, you see, often happen when... when we..."

He ground to a halt under the Emperor's unyielding gaze, and there was silence, filled by an incongruous burst of applause from the theater down below across the Pool of St. Tryphaena.

The Emperor continued to gaze down, with disturbingly steady eyes set in red rings—

——and the Consul and the Tribune were silent——

——and at last the Emperor asked, in a quiet and steady voice,

"Did you kill her?"

The Consul and Tribune were silent for some time, and the Emperor repeated the question in the same detached way:

"Did you kill her?"

"Your clemency, you saw the lady's letter," the Consul said.

"Yes, I saw the letter," the Emperor said, still just as steady. And then he asked, "Did you write it?"

The Consul's voice faltered for a moment. He looked at the Tribune, and at one of the guards (who appeared to be doing his best to look off into the distance as if the distance were so intensely fascinating that he had not heard any of the last few minutes' conversation), and then back at the Emperor, finally managing to squeeze out, "Why would you say that?"

"I don't know." the Emperor replied. "What I've been hearing... I don't even know what her writing looked like. I never—

And then the Emperor's eyes lost their focus. "Oh," he said. The Consul and the Tribune could think of nothing to say.

"She didn't write it," the Emperor said, his eyes still focused on nothing.

"Your clemency," the Consul began, "why—"

"She didn't write it," the Emperor repeated, and now his eyes focused directly on the Consul, "because she couldn't read."

A thick pause followed this statement. Across the Pool of St. Tryphaena, down in the theater, there was a burst of laughter.

The Consul attempted a hypothesis. "Perhaps she... asked a friend to write it for her...." After a few more moments of silence, he added, "?"

"A friend who was willing to write for her, and was not willing to prevent her from..."

The Emperor did not complete the thought, but it had

been completed well enough in everyone's mind.

Another burst of applause drifted up from the theater.

"I don't know what to do," the Emperor said.

After a long interval of silence, broken by an explosive sneeze from the Consul and an answering roar from Jerome, the Consul began to suggest, "Perhaps if your clemency would return to the theater, we could discuss the matter more fully after—"

"I don't know what to do about *you*," said the Emperor. "I don't know what to think. I don't know what to do. I don't know what to know." He did not speak in anger: he had used up his anger over the previous weeks, and now nothing was left but a bottomless well of helpless grief. He could not even make a decision when every indication seemed to be telling him that he had been betrayed in the foulest way he could imagine. The only decision he could come to was to put off coming to his decision.

"Guards," he said, "take these two men to the prison until I decide what to do about them."

The four guards all stopped breathing at once. They were all very well trained, and all their training came down to this: always obey the orders of the Emperor, as mediated through the Consul and the Tribune. And long experience had taught all the palace guards that orders in general originated with the Consul, who mediated the Emperor's intentions by expressing them before the Emperor had to bother with intending them. There was no precedent for an order from the Emperor that went against the interests of the Consul and the Tribune.

The Emperor looked at the lignified guards and began

to wonder whether he really had any imperial power at all.

And he could not be permitted to wonder about that. "The Emperor's will is law," said the Consul. "Guards, you have your orders. It will not be necessary to bind us. Your clemency, we will await your pleasure."

So saying, the Consul, with simple gestures, directed the guards to take their positions, two at the front of him and the Tribune and two behind, and the six men marched eastward along the terrace path, soon disappearing around a curve behind a luxuriant butterfly-push.

The Emperor sank to the ground again. Another burst of applause came up from the theater, and he tried, for the sake of thinking about anything at all, to imagine what might be going on down there. But a grey wall had been erected in front of his mind, and his thoughts could not get through or around it. There was only the mass of present perceptions again: the light breeze, the sounds from the theater below and starlings above, the warm lion leaning against him. They were perceptions, but they refused to come together into meaning. One thing made some sort of sense to him: for a very brief moment the world had belonged to him, and then it was taken away. This he could understand. And there must be a reason for it, but he couldn't think what it would be.

The Consul and the Tribune, meanwhile, marched to the small section of the palace that was used as a prison, and they entered a small but clean cell with two beds, two chairs, and a table; and the door was locked behind them. The Consul made sure of that by locking it himself, and he put the key on a chain around his neck to keep it safe.

CHAPTER 24

THE EMPEROR'S CONSCIENCE

FOR the first time in his life there was no one to guide the Emperor. It was not only that there was no one to tell him what to do, and what it would not be advisable to do: that was hard enough, because he had usually relied on such direction. But even on those few occasions when he had felt full of his imperial self and rebelled and done what he wanted to do, there had been something to rebel against. That gave him direction in itself. Now there was nothing but the void, because the Consul had always been there. He had always been the standard for what was, if not right and wrong, then at least done and not done. And if the Emperor had decided to do what was not done, then at least he knew he was doing it. Now his world had no order. The force that pulled all things back to their natural place was gone.

For quite a long time the Emperor just sat. It was long enough that Jerome had to find a freshly dug flower bed nearby and decide for himself that it was morally equivalent to a sand pit. The sounds from the theater continued for some time, and then after some indefinite period the Emperor realized that there had been no more of them for quite a while. He would have to be somewhere else eventually, although for a while he wondered whether that was indeed so, and whether he might not just stay in the Terrace Garden now and for however much time was left. When he did at last pick himself off the ground and start to move, it was toward the imperial residence, because nothing occurred to him as worth doing except going back to his chamber to sleep. Jerome would have to eat, too; the Emperor thought that, as for himself, it might be interesting to see how never eating again worked out.

But when he came out of the Terrace Garden, the great dome of the Church of the Assumption was right in front of him, and it pulled him toward it—or at least toward the church, since it was necessary for him to turn left and walk up toward the Forum to get there. He had a strong desire, which had come over him all at once, to be in the church.

It was very strange walking up toward the Forum by himself. There were people around him now, but not very close: they kept a respectful distance from the purple border, and perhaps respected the lion on a chain even more.

At the southeast corner of the Forum, opposite the Fountain Court, the Emperor ascended the steps that led to the west front of the church. He was not quite sure what to do when he got to the door: it had never been closed before when he intended to go through it. But it must have a handle for a reason. The Emperor had just reached out to grasp the handle when the great door swung open wide enough to reveal the Archeparch standing behind it.

"Your clemency," he said, bowing exactly as low as

etiquette permitted an Archeparch to bow to an earthly ruler.

"I want to come in," said the Emperor. "Is that all right?"

"The church is always open, your clemency."

"And is it all right if Jerome comes too?"

The Archeparch looked down at the lion. "He won't make a mess on the floor, will he?"

"He's trained. He uses a sand pit."

"Then, since he is also one of God's creatures, he is welcome here." The Archeparch opened the door wider as a visible token of welcome, and the Emperor and his lion came in.

The church was huge when it was empty. At this time of day—it was late afternoon—the light inside was fairly dim, except that there was a brighter patch at the altar from the light streaming in under the dome. The Emperor looked down toward the altar for a moment, and then said the first words that came to him:

"I think I need to make a confession."

"Is there some particular sin you need to confess?" the Archeparch asked.

"Yes. No.—I don't know. I feel sinful, but I don't know what the sin is."

The Archeparch thought for a moment and then said, "Come with me."

So the Archeparch led the Emperor and his lion along the side aisle to the comfortable room where he generally heard the Emperor's confessions. There they both sat in their accustomed seats, and Jerome rubbed his head against the Archeparch's knees until the Archeparch consented to scratch him around the mane, which his fingers continued to do automatically for most of the rest of the conversation.

It began as usual with the Emperor asking for the Archeparch's blessing and confessing that he had sinned. But after that there was a considerable period of silence.

At last the Archeparch suggested, "Suppose you start by telling me what it was that made you think you ought to come here."

"She's dead," the Emperor said instantly.

"Yes," the Archeparch agreed. He did not have to be told who "she" was.

"She's dead because I loved her, but—" He had to stop a moment to control his quavering voice. "But I still don't know why it was wrong to love her."

"But you are sure it was wrong?"

"It must have been wrong! How could I be punished like this if it wasn't wrong?"

"That is a difficult question. Even the holy Job asked it, and he had to be content with imperfect understanding. But let us ask ourselves a few other questions. Did you lust after her flesh?"

"I loved her flesh. Her flesh—it was *her*. Wasn't it? She was so beautiful, and—and I loved her for what she said, and for what she thought, and for what she did. And when she was in my bed, and we— you know, when she taught me about love with, with the body, that was so holy and good that I can't call it a sin. It made her so happy. It would be… It would be like calling God a sinner."

"I see. But perhaps if you could describe in detail what she did with you, leaving nothing out, and making sure especially to describe her legs, we could see whether there is, in fact, any sin to be found..."

"I couldn't," the Emperor said with tears rolling down his cheeks. "I just can't—— I can't even think about it. She was so beautiful and so good!" He covered his eyes for a few moments, which gave the Archeparch time to feel ashamed of himself. Then the Emperor looked up and said, in a more composed voice, "You heard that I put the Consul and the Tribune in prison?"

"I heard," said the Archeparch. "Such things are not kept secret for long."

"I don't know what to do. I heard them talking, and it sounded— it was— I think they might have killed her. And why? How could...? But the note— she was— she didn't write it, and I was so stupid, because how could she have written it? But did they do it? Or did they make her do it? And what will I do if they did? I have to be their judge—but I'm not strong enough! How could I be, when they were always my strength? And if I judge that they must die, then my sin will have killed them, too. But what can I do? I don't know anything. I don't understand anything."

The Archeparch let some silence pass before suggesting, "Perhaps you ought to pray."

"You mean—a few Our Fathers and I'm absolved?" the Emperor asked, and there was a slight tinge of involuntary contempt in his tone.

"No. The Our Father is a model prayer, meant to teach us to pray, but not to supplant our own prayers. It teaches us to speak directly to God."

"But he doesn't talk back, does he?"

"To great saints, he does. Sometimes to madmen. But for poor sinners like us, he listens."

"What do I do?"

"Just go out there, perhaps in front of the altar, and talk to God. Ask for help. Tell him what you need. It's what I would do."

"And does he—answer?"

"God always answers prayers. But usually he wants you to figure out what the answer is."

That struck the Emperor as a bit hard. But he had no other ideas, and he did have a strong feeling that sin was hanging around his neck like a millstone. He walked out into the church and slowly approached the altar. He stood and looked at the multitude of images of saints watching him from every direction, and he felt embarrassed to be in their company. Those were men and women who knew how to pray. All he knew how to do was say the Our Father as many times as he was directed to say it. But he felt very strongly that he needed something here, and perhaps the Archeparch was right.

It was probably best to kneel, so the Emperor got down on his knees. Jerome, of course, took this as a sign that his friend must need a lion, and pressed himself up against the Emperor, lying down with his head in the optimum ear-scratching position. So with one hand thus occupied, the Emperor tried to begin a conversation with God.

"Well," he said—and then he added, "God," so that anyone else listening would know to whom the conversation was addressed, "I'm here because... Well, the Archeparch said I should talk to you, and he knows you a lot better than I do, and—and so I thought I'd just say... I thought I'd say... I loved her, God! I thought love was good! Why did she die? Why was it wrong to love her?

Why was there no way for me to be happy? And now that I'm here, now that she's gone, how can I live? I don't want to die, but I don't want to live either. I don't want to *be*. And it was all because..."

Now, the Emperor did not actually *hear* God speaking to him, and he was not at all sure that he had not simply let his mind go and think up thoughts it hadn't thought before. But suddenly he had a name for his sin, and he thought he'd try it out.

"I was *proud*. It was all because I was proud. I was so proud that I thought I could have everything my own way. I was so proud I thought I could *not be Emperor*. I thought I could have simple things, simple happiness. I thought I could have joy for myself. And I forgot that joy isn't for Emperors!"

He had to stop for a few moments, because the flood-gates of grief were threatening to open again. But he was able to compose himself enough to go on.

"And I repent, God! I'm sorry I ever thought of being common. I'm sorry I ever thought of being ordinary. I'm sorry I ever thought of being anything but what you made me. Couldn't that be enough? I know I don't deserve anything, but I've learned! I've learned! And I know there aren't miracles anymore, but... I wanted her so much! I know that's no excuse. And I know she's with you, and that's better, and... Take good care of her, God. Please. And if somehow you could tell her I still love her..."

Here he had to stop, because he was overcome by tears. So was the Archeparch, who had been watching and listening unobserved from a dark corner in the south transept.

But after a little while, the Emperor felt surprisingly

lightened. He had lost a weight that had been pressing on him. He stood up, the tears still drying on his cheeks; he gave Jerome one more scratch; and the two of them walked out the great west door together. The Emperor even managed to operate the handle all by himself.

The Archeparch, who had watched the Emperor and his lion leave, turned to find the Consul and the Tribune waiting behind him.

"Have you anything to tell us?" the Consul asked.

"Yes, said the Archeparch. "You're both excommunicated till I say otherwise."

CHAPTER 25

THE GHOST

THE Emperor feigned sleep very early that night. The moon was getting bright again, and it was time to visit the Forest of Arches.

It had not occurred to him until now that he wanted to visit the Forest of Arches by night again. But now something had lifted from him, and he felt that he could do it. It was not that he was happy: in fact, if it had been necessary for him to articulate what he was feeling, he might have said that for the first time he was able to be properly sad. He shed some tears as he sat on the altar with Jerome's great head in his lap and remembered how she had loved the beauty of the place. As he walked back he remembered her saying that she would love to wander here for all eternity if she had to be a ghost. He even called her name three or four times, but of course there was no answer, although he was sure other spirits were about: he caught a glimpse of the little round figure he sometimes saw at the edges of shadows, and there were soft footsteps now and then. It made him sad to think of her, and it was good to be sad instead of empty. He came back and climbed in his window and slept soundly the rest of the night.

The next morning, after his morning breakfast (the valets had given up on the tonic, which was not doing the promenade any good), the Emperor thought he ought to visit the Consul and the Tribune in prison and see whether he could figure out what to do with them. But he had a philosophy lesson in the morning, and he went through with it because the alternative was going to the prison to see the Consul and the Tribune, which he did not want to do. Iamblichus talked about geometry as a proof of the existence of a world of ideals, of which the material world is but a shadow; the Emperor did not ask any difficult questions, so that Iamblichus enjoyed the lesson more thoroughly than any lesson in recent memory.

After that the Emperor did summon up the determination to visit his prisoners. It was hard to think of them that way: his prisoners. To think of them that way was to remind himself that he would have to make some decision sooner or later. He would have to determine their fate, and he had no real practice in determining fates. Whenever there had been a difficult decision, the Consul and the Tribune had told him what he ought to do. And he could go back to that simple and comfortable world right now. He could simply let them go and tell them there was no evidence that they had done anything wrong, and then they could go back to telling him what was done and what was not done. It would be easy. But if they had betrayed him in some way, and it was difficult to imagine (having heard what he had heard) that they had not, then he would know that his whole life was a lie.

He had to ask one of his guards the way to the prison.

Prisoners had always been brought to him when he had business with then, which was usually pardoning them. He had never gone to them until now. He was pleased to find that the prison was a clean and comfortable place: it had worried him to imagine the Consul and the Tribune in dungeon cells with horrible crawling things skittering along the walls, but this was in fact part of the servants' quarters for the imperial residence, and kept as tidy as the rest of it. Two guards flanked the door, which had been opened in anticipation of his arrival, as had the inner door of the prisoners' cell (the Emperor was used to his doings being anticipated), and the two prisoners, seated at the simple table, rose to receive their imperial guest, and the imperial lion who accompanied him.

"Your clemency," said the Consul with a bow, and the Tribune did the same.

"Are you comfortable?" the Emperor asked.

Jerome rubbed himself against the Tribune, who began to sniffle.

"Are you getting enough to eat?"

The Tribune answered, "Oh, lots," which the Consul quickly amended to "More than we might have expected in our circumstances."

"Good," said the Emperor. He stood for a moment looking at the floor, which looked like a floor. Then he asked, "Did you kill her?"

Both men let an extended moment of silence pass; then the Consul answered, "No." The Tribune added a sneeze.

It was not a satisfying answer, but the Emperor realized that no answer could have been satisfying. The hesitation had made him doubt the truth of the answer, but would an instant denial have been any more convincing? —He pulled the worn papyrus out of his robe and asked, "Who wrote this letter?" He laid it down on the table beside the Consul.

The Consul only glanced at it and answered, "I can't say."

"It's the kind of ink and the kind of papyrus you use for palace documents, isn't it?"

"It appears to be," said the Consul without looking at the letter,

"Why? asked the Emperor.

"The ink is not kept under guard," said the Consul.

The Emperor accepted this answer because there was no arguing with it. He hesitated to ask the next question, because it was unpleasant, but he could not think of anything else to ask that would get him any information: "Did you tell her to kill herself?"

"No," the Consul replied.

"Did you *persuade* her to kill herself?"

The Consul allowed another uncomfortable silence to pass before answering, "No."

The Emperor looked from the Consul to the Tribune. The Tribune looked a little more fragile, and perhaps a sudden burst of rage could have broken him; but the Emperor didn't have a sudden burst of rage in him, nor could he even imagine breaking the Tribune, or wanting to break the Tribune. It was a horrible and distasteful thought. Jerome was making the poor man suffer enough already.

And so the Emperor and Jerome left, having accomplished nothing, and when they were gone the Consul closed and locked the door.

"I told you it would be a disaster," said the Tribune,

"But," said the Consul, "I have great confidence in the moonlight."

"It had better work," the Tribune said, "because things can hardly get any worse. You realize, if he has us executed, the Sultan will kill us."

"We do not speak that name," the Consul said automatically. But he did not dispute the assertion.

Nothing happened the rest of the day, although even without the Consul and the Tribune the nothing happened very elaborately and took up a great deal of time. When the Emperor was being readied for bed, he seriously considered telling the imperial bedchamber orchestra not to bother, because he was going out for a walk by moonlight. Who would stop him? But someone might; and besides, he remembered how hard the musicians worked, and how disappointed they would be if they didn't play. It was best to let them do their job for half an hour or so as usual.

When he did slip out (not forgetting a bit of bread for Alexius, who seemed undisturbed by the lion), the moon was shining bright. It would be full in another day or so, but its illumination was certainly more than adequate for his purposes. The spirits seemed to be out in force tonight: he heard soft footsteps frequently, though they always stopped if he looked in the direction of the sound.

The Emperor spent some time in his little chamber scratching behind Jerome's ears and trying to figure things out, but he could not even come to any definite conclusion about what the things were that needed to be figured out. He needed to know what to do, but what to do about what? If he was accusing the Consul and the

Tribune of murder, then there would have to be a trial. But was he accusing them of murder? Did he want to hold a trial and be their judge?

Eventually he started back, not having decided anything. And it was while walking across the great roofless basilica that he saw the ghost.

At first it was just an indistinct movement in the shadows by the southern wall, not much different from many other indistinct movements he thought he might have seen. But then it floated out into the moonlight, and the Emperor stopped and stood dead still.

Ethereal billows surrounded the apparition. A cool breeze was blowing from the west, enough to set the spiritual robes in motion. She—for right away the Emperor could see that it was a feminine spirit—was drifting toward him, the moon above and behind her, the light giving her flowing robes an internal luminance as it filtered through them, so that she was outlined in a pale glow. He could not see the face yet. He stood as still as if his feet had been nailed there, and only when his body sent him some distress signals did he realize that he had forgotten to breathe. Still she came closer, until she stopped about three paces in front of him and uttered two words:

"My love."

"Pulcheria!" It came out as a whisper that carried all his breath with it.

"Don't touch me," the spirit said, sounding for a moment like the lively woman he had known. Then, in a more ethereally spiritual voice, she continued, "It is not permitted to reach across the gap between the worlds."

"You came here," the Emperor said. "You said you wanted to, and..."

"I came here to right a grievous wrong. You must not accuse anyone of what I did of my own volition." The spirit pronounced the word "volition" carefully, as if it were not a very familiar one.

The Emperor felt a surge of strangely conflicting passions—relief and awe and sadness and fright and confusion. "But who wrote the letter, Pulcheria?"

"I had a servant write it." Jerome, who had been sitting next to his friend, now stood.

"But your servant knew what was in it and didn't stop you?"

"She—she couldn't read."

"She could write but she couldn't read?"

"More or less. I don't know. It was hard to—— Jerome!"

The lion had rubbed against the ghost with his usual enthusiastic force, and she was thrown off balance. By instinct the Emperor leaped forward and grasped her arm —an arm made of warm, soft flesh.

"Pulcheria!" he almost shouted, pulling her to him and himself toward her. "You're still alive!"

"For now," she responded. Then she fell on his shoulder and burst into tears.

CHAPTER 26

A REVELATION FROM THE SPIRIT WORLD

IT WAS some time before it seemed appropriate for either of them to speak. The dead do not often come back to life. The love he had lost was in his arms, and he was afraid to breathe. If he so much as changed the position of his hands on her back, she might be gone again. Jerome rubbed himself against their hips for a while, but the two were so still for so long that he gave up and sprawled on the ground to wait for someone to remember the lion.

Pulcheria was the first to speak, and the first words she whispered were "I'm sorry." After a while, she whispered then again, and then added, "I couldn't let anything happen to you."

"Nothing will happen to us," the Emperor said softly into her ear. "I won't let you go. You'll be my Empress."

"That can't happen," she said, raising her head from his shoulder.

"It can," he insisted. "'The Emperor's will is law!'"

"It won't be allowed, Something will be done. I won't be— I mean.. they'll—"

"No one can do anything to you. I'll hold on and never

let you go, I'll keep—"

"You don't understand. They'd find a way."

"Then we'll leave. We'll go somewhere else."

"You can't—"

"I'm the Emperor! If the palace is against me, then I'll turn the whole Empire against the palace!

"It won't happen! You can't do that!"

"Why not? You're worth anything. You give me the courage to do anything—"

"But not that! That can't be—"

"Yes, even that! Why not that?"

"Because there is no Empire!"

This silenced him long enough to let her continue for a moment:

"If I'm going to die anyway, I might as well die for the unthinkable. I might as well be the one who tells you the truth."

"Of course there's an Empire," the Emperor insisted. "I appoint governors for the provinces. I just appointed a new general for the Aspersian war."

"It's a show. You're a show. And I thought that was all you were, but then I met you, and you were so good…"

The Emperor was not ready to understand yet. "Do you mean that I'm not really the ruler, and the Consul does what he wants?" This was not far from what he had always secretly suspected.

"No—no, oh, I love you so much, and I can't—— There's just no Empire at all. The Empire ends at the wall of the palace. The palace is all there is. The Sultan's great-grandfather conquered everything else."

"The Sultan is my most loyal vassal," the Emperor said helplessly.

"I'm sorry," Pulcheria whispered. Then she continued in a normal voice: "All my life I've known that the one unthinkable crime is to tell the Emperor the truth. Everyone knows that. Everyone accepts it. But I never even wondered whether it was wrong to lie to you. I'm sorry. I didn't—— I'm sorry."

"I don't believe you," the Emperor said. And then, after a moment's thought, he added, "I do believe you." He held her tighter. "You're the only one who's ever told me the truth about anything."

"I'm sorry," she repeated yet again.

"Walk with me," he said; and the two of them began to stroll slowly and aimlessly toward the northwest, Pulcheria's ethereal robes billowing around them in the breeze, his arm around her shoulders, hers around his waist. For some time they were silent, and the Emperor was aware that, as soon as he spoke, something would end. Possibly it would be his life.

But eventually he did speak. "Who made you pretend to…"

"The Consul and the Tribune, and they were really being—well, not kind to me, but the choice was being boiled in oil or making you think I'd killed myself. And when they showed me that you might be in danger if I didn't… I knew that things might happen to you, you see? So I said I'd do it if you could know that I loved you. They put me in a little house in the city outside the palace. And then when you put them in prison, they came and got me, and—"

"They came and got you? I thought they were in prison!"

"Well, they are, but they can sort of…get out when

they need to."

Of course they could. If they were just allowing him to play at being Emperor, then they were just allowing him to play at putting them in prison. "And they made you come back from the dead."

"I told them I couldn't. I told them it would kill me to see you again and lie to you. And..."

The Emperor filled in: "And they persuaded you."

"The Consul said the cauldron would be a less met-a-phor-ic-al kind of death. And I really didn't want you to kill them for murdering me when... Although in a way they did murder me, but not really."

They had reached the corner of the great basilica, and since they had no destination they simply turned and strolled in the opposite direction.

After another period of silence, the Emperor asked, "Why am I here, then? Why is there...me? Why is there an Emperor?"

"It's what the Sultan wants. I don't know why. It just is. We have to keep the Empire going, even though it's only this palace, because if we don't, the Consul loses his head, and the Tribune, and they make sure a lot of other heads are missing first. And I suppose it's going to hap-pen now, because I loved you too much to keep lying to you." And then she corrected herself. "No, they'll make you go on somehow. I have to die, but you have to go on."

"No," the Emperor said, and he stopped suddenly, so that Jerome had to turn around and walk back. "Pul-cheria, even if the Empire really is only this palace, even if it were only a closet, would you share it with me? I won't go on without you, and the Consul can do his worst, but with you I might be able to do something."

"I don't see what you can do," Pulcheria said.

"But you have a choice. Give up and die, or dare everything and maybe not die. I don't know what will happen, but will you be with me?"

"I don't have a choice," she replied. "I made my choice when I gave you any word. I went back on it once; I don't have the strength to do it again."

"Then I have you and I have Jerome," the Emperor said, and those two allies gave him a sudden burst of confidence. A miracle had happened; perhaps there were more miracles to be expected. "Pulcheria, before you knew me, what would you have done if the Emperor gave you an order?"

"I'd have obeyed, of course. No one ever actually got orders directly from you, but if it had happened, we couldn't have disobeyed."

"Then let's see how much of an Emperor I can be."

CHAPTER 27

THE TRIAL

THE Archeparch was very much annoyed to be awakened from such a dream. Already the theme of it was dissolving from his memory; but there had been a number of beautiful young women with legs like alabaster pillars, and the insistent pounding coming from the front of his residence had deprived him of their company. When he found out what young hooligan was responsible—well, he was a pious and charitable man, so the fellow would probably be let off with nothing more than a severe flogging, which would be administered in a spirit of fatherly correction, and would continue until the presumptuous little weasel had had the stuffings corrected out of him.

At last the noise ceased, and the Archeparch lay in bed for a while contemplating the degraded condition of youth these days, and the possibility of restoring some degree of respect and civilized behavior through a program of regular floggings. But then there was light in the chamber: his doorman was standing there holding a little lamp, in the flickering light of which the poor man's face looked like a mask of horror from the old tragedies. He made his announcement in a high, dry-throated voice:

"The Emperor to see you, your piety."

And the Emperor came right in behind him, not giving the Archeparch any time to put on his ecclesiastical dignity.

"I'm going to need you," the Emperor said. "There's going to be a trial."

"A trial?" the Archeparch repeated.

"The Consul and the Tribune are being tried for murder."

"For murder?" the Archeparch repeated.

"Get dressed and come to the Hall of Lions now."

"Now?" the Archeparch repeated.

But the Emperor was already striding out of the chamber, with the poor confused doorman running after him to make sure he never ran out of light.

The Archeparch, sitting in the dark, called for his valet. He called again, and yet again, before the old man appeared with his own lamp—actually with admirable alacrity, but the Archeparch was feeling very impatient.

"Light the lamps and get me dressed," said the Archeparch. "I'm going to a trial."

The valet immediately began lighting the lamps from his own lamp. "Will we be requiring our Sunday best?" he asked.

"The best I have," the Archeparch replied, throwing off the bedclothes. "Something suitable for my funeral."

The guards at the prison were awake, because they were on night duty, so of course it was their duty to be awake. It was true that a pair of comfortable-looking cots had recently been slept in by somebody, but by the time the Emperor's deliberately noisy footsteps had reached the prison section, the two men were standing in front of the cell door in the attitude of men who had very definitely been awake and alert all this time.

"The prisoners are to be brought to the Hall of Lions at once," the Emperor declared.

The guards looked quite stricken. "At once?" one of them asked in a rather squeaky voice.

The Emperor had mercy on them. "Well, as soon as they can be retrieved from...whatever corner of the cell they've got into."

He turned and left the guards to breathe again. But they had not got in more than about a breach and a half before the Emperor reappeared to add,

"And have the executioner brought, too."

The guards stared in loose-jawed horror.

"In case the prisoners are found guilty," the Emperor explained. Then he was gone.

It took some time for the jaws to close after that, and a little longer for the guards to sort out which one was to fetch the Consul and the Tribune and which one the executioner. Neither was an assignment to be anticipated with delight.

Within an hour, the Emperor was seated on his throne in the Hall of Lions, wearing the purple robe of Adrianus XIII and looking as imperial as he could manage. The robe was just as itchy as ever, but the Emperor would put up with the itching for the sake of the dignity it conferred. He got his last few scratches in before the great doors opened, and then watched the interesting parade of the Archeparch in his Sunday best, followed by the Consul and the Tribune, followed by the two night-duty guards, followed by the little round executioner with his peculiar rolling gait, all gradually appearing from the darkness that filled most of the hall. It was very different from the usual imperial audience: no lines of guards stood along the walls (the Emperor would not have known how to summon them even if he had thought they were necessary), and the many lampstands that had been fetched from neighboring halls and chambers could hardly begin to eat up the darkness. But Jerome did roar when the Consul came near, so the trial was in session.

"The prisoners are present and the lion has roared," said the Emperor. "The trial has begun."

"Your clemency," the Consul said, "this procedure may be somewhat irregular. If we could perhaps—"

"It is irregular," said the Emperor, "because it is not usual to have murders among the senatorial class."

"But perhaps a more regular procedure would be to—"

"The Emperor judges, sentences, pardons, elevates, and degrades," the Emperor declared. "I am judging now, which is a perfectly regular part of the Emperor's duties."

The Tribune sneezed, adding a punctuation mark to the Emperor's decisive statement.

"We shall begin with the testimony of the chief witness," said the Emperor. "I am the chief witness, so I shall give my testimony. On the day of the spectacle, you, Consul, said, and the words are etched on my memory, "It had become necessary that she should cease to exist." You were referring, I believe, to the late Empress. Is my memory correct?"

The Consul considered his reply for a moment, and then spoke carefully: "Your clemency's memory is doubtless more accurate than mine."

"And as I recall, my memory being admitted as accurate, the Consul's remark came in response to a statement by you, Tribune, to the effect that getting rid of the floor-scrubber, as one or the other of you called her, had been a greater mistake than letting me have her. Forgive me if my memory does not reproduce the words exactly. Is my summary of your statement accurate?"

The Tribune sneezed, and Jerome roared in reply. Since the Emperor received no other reply, he decided to take his accuracy as confirmed.

"Now," he continued, retrieving a rumpled papyrus from his robe, "I present as evidence this letter, supposedly written by the late Empress before her tragic death. Yet the late Empress could not read. How did this letter come to be written?"

The Consul glanced down at the Tribune, and then replied, "We are of the opinion that she must have dictated it to a servant."

"Yes," said the Emperor, "that would be an explanation. So it is still your assertion that the late Empress took her own life?"

"It is," said the Consul. The Tribune nodded tensely, wiping his nose with a cloth.

"And you saw her dead?"

"Unfortunately so, your clemency," said the Consul, "and may I never see such a sight again."

The Emperor turned to the Tribune. "And you?"

"Oh, yes. It was awful."

"Archeparch," the Emperor said, "you came to the scene of the unfortunate death. Was the Empress dead when you arrived?"

"Yes," the Archeparch answered after a moment's

hesitation.

"Which is interesting," said the Emperor, "since the Consul told me you gave her the last rites."

The Archeparch looked at the Consul, and then turned back to the Emperor. "Clearly the Consul misunderstood. I did pray for her soul, of course."

"So you all three agree that she was quite definitely dead when you last saw her, and that she had taken her own life."

"Yes," they all answered at once, the Tribune adding a sneeze for emphasis.

"Then it appears that I may have to render a verdict of suicide," the Emperor declared. "However, there is one more witness to be heard from."

The three men looked at the Emperor expectantly; the executioner, who had remained at some distance off to the side in the shadows, bore an expression that was unreadable behind his immense black mustache. When the Emperor had remained silent for some time, the three realized that his gaze was directed toward the back of the hall; and one by one they turned and saw the ghost.

The far end of the hall was almost completely dark, the lamps being concentrated near the throne; but the few exhausted and enervated rays of light that made it back there caught on an ethereal form slowly moving forward out of the darkness. She seemed to float, her loose robes drifting beside and behind her, and there was a dread silence during her long progress from the darkness into the dim light.

At last she stopped, some distance yet from the group at the front of the hall, and gazed steadily at the Emperor.

"O blessed spirit," said the Emperor in his best tragic-actor intonation, "what message hast thou brought from the world beyond the grave?"

"Call me not blessed," the spirit responded in equally formal diction, "for I am doomed to wander the abode of mortals until a grievous wrong has been righted."

The Consul, the Tribune, and the Archeparch all watched the ghost with varying expressions of wonder and apprehension.

"What wrong, Spirit," the Emperor asked, "binds thee to earth?"

"My death, O Emperor." The spirit's right hand slowly rose on a rigid arm. "My death, a foul murder, and these two men the murderers!"

Her fully outstretched arm supported two fingers pointing straight at the Consul and the Tribune.

"My lady——" the Consul began.

The Emperor interrupted. "O spirit, dost thou accuse these men of thy murder?"

"These two men," said the spirit; "I accuse these two men, who are directly responsible for my death."

"But—" the Consul began. He turned to the Emperor. "But, your clemency, we certainly are not!"

The Emperor frowned a terrifying imperial frown. "You would dare impugn the veracity of a spirit from the world beyond?"

"But surely—"

"The spirit of the victim has spoken!" The Emperor rose from his throne. "The crime is murder!"

"But this is false," the Consul cried. "This is—"

"You deny a revelation from the spirit world?"

"Surely you can see—"

"We have the voice of the victim herself!" the Emperor declared. "The testimony cannot be doubted!"

"But we never—"

"The sentence for murder is—"

"But this is not a spirit!"

The silence that followed this declaration would have been more impressive if the Tribune had not at that moment lost his long battle with a sneeze.

Slowly the Emperor stepped down from the imperial dais. Both the Consul and the Tribune stood frozen as he approached—the Archeparch, meanwhile, discreetly adding some distance between himself and them without appearing to move his feet. At last (for it seemed to take a long while) the Emperor was standing right in front of the two men.

"If this is not a spirit," he demanded quietly, "then what is she?"

The Consul and the Tribune both hesitated for some time. But in the end the Tribune spoke the only answer that could possibly save his life: "A living woman, your clemency."

The Emperor addressed himself to the Consul: "Do you concur?"

The Consul's voice was not very confident. "I must."

"Empress," said the Emperor, looking at Pulcheria and holding out his hand to her, "is it true that you are not a ghost, but a woman of flesh and blood?"

She approached with as much dignity as she was capable of and took his offered hand. "Yes, my beloved Emperor," she said in something close to a senatorial accent.

"And you were never dead?"

"I was never dead."

"Well, then," the Emperor said, turning back to the Consul and the Tribune, "this changes things considerably. Where there is no death, there can be no crime of murder. Isn't that right?"

"Perfectly correct, your clemency," the Consul said with obvious relief.

"Instead," the Emperor continued, "the crime is presumption."

"Presumption?" the Tribune squeaked.

"You plotted to thwart the Emperor's express will. Presumption! You threatened to kill the woman I had told you I intended to make my Empress. Presumption! You forced her to participate in an elaborate deception under threat of death. Presumption! You lied directly to your Emperor and told me she was dead. Presumption! When I began to suspect you, you concocted another elaborate scheme to deceive me. Presumption! At every step you attempted to impose your will instead of mine on the Empire. Presumption!"

"But——" the Consul began, and then realized that for once he had no more words beyond that one.

"The penalty for presumption," the Emperor declared, "is boiling in oil. Guards, secure these two men. Executioner, prepare the cauldron. Archeparch, see to their confessions."

CHAPTER 28

THE CAULDRON

IT TAKES some time to get a cauldron of oil up to the proper temperature. Not until dawn would the oil be ready, the Emperor was informed; so the double execution was scheduled for dawn. Word had spread in that miraculous way gossip has of spreading, and already a crowd had started to gather in the Forum, many carrying torches, which creates a festive atmosphere in which to share rumors and speculations. Some were of the opinion that the condemned had merited this punishment a long time ago. Others thought it was a shame it had to come to this. Some said it was good to see the young Emperor showing some strength of character at last. And here and there, a few could be found who dared whisper what the whole crowd was thinking: perhaps the world is coming to an end.

The Consul and the Tribune were sitting on the platform, their hands bound behind them. It had come down to a question of whether the guards were to obey the Emperor's explicit commands, or defy him and accept the Consul and the Tribune as the real authorities. There was no precedent for such a decision, but the very name of

Emperor made it for the guards. If the Emperor spoke to them directly, his will must be law.

The Emperor, meanwhile, was with Pulcheria, who told him how she had thought of him every day in the little house beyond the city wall to which she had been banished after her supposed suicide.

"I've always wanted a little house," the Emperor told her. "I always wanted to be a little man in a little house where nobody bothered me."

"You probably didn't want the one with roaches as big as your foot."

He thought about that for a moment. "I suppose not."

"I've been little all my life. People bother you a lot when you're little."

"Do they? I never thought about it. I suppose people just bother people no matter who the people are."

Pulcheria leaned against his shoulder, her hand gripping his, and finally, after a long silence, said quietly, "You realize the Sultan may kill us both."

"If you die, I die with you," the Emperor told her. "But if he wants an Emperor, then he can have one on my terms."

She pressed her head into him harder. "I'll know you loved me, at least. It would almost be good to die knowing that."

"Yes," the Emperor agreed. "But it would be a whole lot better to live."

And as he spoke, he noticed that the rosy fingers of dawn had just begun to reach above the horizon.

By this time the crowd in the Forum had swollen to include just about every inhabitant of the palace, and the mood was celebratory. If the world was going to end, the people were going to enjoy the show. The noise level was high enough that it took some time for silence to fall when the Emperor appeared on the platform, with the Empress beside him, and Jerome beside her. But after everyone had pointed out to his neighbor that the former floor-scrubber was wearing a purple-bordered robe, the crowd began to wonder whether the Emperor might have something interesting to say. One by one the voices dropped out, until at last the Emperor had a very attentive audience.

Now he had to figure out what to say.

The crowd was dead silent, and the sound of the cauldron bubbling, inaudible before, seemed quite loud.

"Uh," said the Emperor. But when he didn't know what to say to begin with, his position at least gave him some ceremony to get him started. "The Emperor's compliments to the Senate and people. We— we have a bit of a... These two men stand before you, well actually they sit before you, convicted of presumption in that they misled your Emperor, meaning me, and devised a scheme to prevent my marriage to the Empress, in defiance of my will, which I've always been told is law. So you know what the penalty is for presumption. I mean, there it is."

He pointed to the cauldron, and allowed the sound of it to fill the silence for a few moments. Then he continued:

"However, henceforth the will of the Empress is law as well. And it is the will of the Empress that these men should not die..."

There was a rumble from the crowd, the sound of a mob trying to decide whether to applaud or protest.

"It seems," the Emperor began, a little louder—"It seems that there are certain circumstances, which the

Empress has urged in extenuation, that suggest laudable motives in their conduct, mistaken though it was. And so, they will be spared—"

A few in the crowd took this as a signal for applause.

"If—" the Emperor continued, and the applause withered—"If certain conditions are met, which the Empress and I have agreed on."

He reached into his robe and pulled out a worn papyrus; but it was not the one he was looking for, and it took some fumbling before he found a much fresher-looking sheet, which he unrolled.

"These are the conditions," he said, reading from the sheet. "First, Pulcheria to be Empress, with authority equal to mine.

"Second, no one ever to be boiled in oil ever again or else. This point is particularly important to the Empress.

"Third, all the meat Jerome the lion wants, to be provided from the personal store of the Empress and Emperor. This point is particularly important to Jerome.

"Fourth, be nice to servants and workers in the lower orders and don't boil them in oil ever.

"Fifth, the purple robe of Adrianus XIII to be retired to an honorable place in the historical collections in the treasury, and a pair of new robes in purple silk to be provided as soon as possible.

"And sixth, no musicians in the bridal chamber on our wedding night.

"These are the conditions. And now, Empress..."

Pulcheria turned and walked three slow steps to the Consul and the Tribune. In a very clear voice, audible to the back of the Forum, she announced, "I pardon you."

There was some murmuring from the crowd.

The Emperor took his place beside the Empress. "If you accept that she has the authority to pardon you, then you're free," he told the two prisoners. "If not, you can have the cauldron if you wish."

"We accept it," the Tribune said instantly.

The Consul, after a very slight moment of hesitation, nodded his agreement.

The Emperor looked at the Empress and smiled. "Give the command," he told her in a voice that was little more than a whisper.

"Guards," said the Empress, "release these men. They're pardoned, and, uh, that's that."

"And they resume their duties and stations," the Emperor added.

A bit of applause began toward the front of the mob and billowed outward until, as the Consul and the Tribune rose free and rubbed their unbound wrists, it had grown to a cheer. It was perhaps not as enthusiastic a cheer as it would have been if the crowd had been given a good execution, but it was at least a cheer of the sort a crowd gives when it feels as if it owes somebody a cheer.

As the cheering continued, the Consul took the opportunity to speak to the Emperor: "You realize, I suppose— since you seem to be informed as to the state of affairs— that the Sultan may have our heads."

"I'm sure my most loyal vassal will be content with this arrangement," said the Emperor. "And beheading's better than boiling in oil."

The Consul nodded, and glanced over at the executioner. It was impossible to read the little round man's expression, but his mustache seemed a little wider.

As the cheering subsided, the Emperor raised his

hands and addressed the crowd once more.

"Now that we have made these arrangements, as I think I can call then, one more thing remains. The formal wedding that will unite me to my Empress has not yet taken place. It will be today at three hours past noon in the Church of the Assumption, followed by a wedding feast for everyone here in the Forum. Consul, Tribune, make all the necessary arrangements."

This time the cheer was definitely enthusiastic. The Empress smiled broadly and waved to the crowd.

The Consul looked down at the Tribune and said, "All the necessary arrangements in half a day..."

"It's not too late for the cauldron, is it?" asked the Tribune.

But in fact the wedding and the feast both were magnificent, because all that was needed to make them magnificent was a large crowd to declare them magnificent. The wedding itself required only the Emperor, the Empress, the Archeparch, and the church, all of which were ready; the feast consisted of whatever could be brought out of the imperial stores and deep-fried in a hurry.

And much later, when the crowds had straggled off to rest or hold post-celebration celebrations of their own, the Empress and the Emperor retired to the imperial bedchamber, where, in the process of preparing for their own celebration, the Emperor found the rumpled papyrus in his discarded robe.

"I suppose I don't need this anymore," he said.

"What is it?" Pulcheria asked, tossing aside her own robe.

"It's the letter they told me was from you. The one you didn't write."

"What does it say?" She was embracing him from behind and resting her chin on his shoulder.

"I could never read past the first few lines. I couldn't get rid of it, because it was all I had of you, but I couldn't read it."

"Read it to me. I want to know whether he kept his promise."

The Emperor was already thinking of things he'd much rather do than read. But he would not deny his Empress' command. "Well, it starts like this:

" 'My love, I have seen on sober reflection the impossibility of our union, and I understand how disastrous it must prove for our Empire. And yet so sincere was I in my protestations of love that I am certain I could not have lived without you. I beg you'—this is where I always had to stop—'I beg you not to take my death too much to heart, though in the short time I have known you I have come to understand how much it will grieve you. If I could in any way have spared you this grief, I would have done so, for you do not deserve it. Believe me that I have acted as I have done only to spare you a much greater and more lasting grief. My last thoughts are of you, my beloved, and when you remember me, remember that I loved you more than life itself.' "

Pulcheria held her husband tighter. "He did keep his promise," she said. "He promised you would know that I loved you, and he wrote the letter I would have written if I had written it. I mean... you know what I mean."

She kissed his shoulder, and the Emperor turned and held her in his arms and pressed his lips to hers, and the music rose in a crescendo of passionate melody——

The Emperor broke away. "Are there musicians in here?"

The music created to a halt, and there was a moment of thick silence.

"Tell them to play 'The Lost Shepherdess,'" the Empress said.

So the music began again, and once again the Empress embraced her Emperor.

"You can't have everything you want, I suppose," she murmured in his ear.

"I already have everything I want," he replied. "Everything in the world. But do you think the world exists outside our perceptions?"

She laughed, partly at the incongruity of the question and partly as a reaction to an unexpectedly delightful caress. "What do you think?"

"Right now I think our perceptions are enough." And that was all he had to say at the time. For all he knew, he might have only this one night left to live, but he could be happy for one night.

CHAPTER 29

THE EMPRESS

SLOWLY, and with a sound of groaning hidden parts enlivened here and there by sudden clangs and pops of bronze, the pair of great doors swung open, the changing angles of the shadows playing with the forms of the tremendous lion reliefs. When at last the doors had come to a stop fully open, the Consul and the Tribune, their heads bowed, stepped through the doorway and began their march across the long series of lion mosaics on the floor, looking neither to the left nor to the right, and certainly not ahead of then. Above all things, the etiquette of the imperial court must be preserved.

The two men slowed in step as they neared the imperial dais, and they stopped on the same foot, as always, just in front of the mosaic of the Emperor Adrianus XVII. And at that moment the lion roared.

The Consul and the Tribune looked up. The Guild of Joiners and the Guild of Carvers had done magnificent work, and a new double throne sat on the dais. It was occupied by the Empress and the Emperor in splendid purple silk.

The Empress spoke: "The compliments of the Empress and the Emperor to the Senate and the People."

There was an almost undetectable moment of hesitation before the Consul replied, "The greetings of the Senate to the Empress and the Emperor, the bearers of their burdens."

The Tribune added, "The greetings of the People to the... Empress and Emperor, the...guardians of their rights." The Tribune's mind did not adapt as quickly as the Consul's, and old habits took some conscious effort to modify.

After that there was a slightly awkward silence, and then the Emperor whispered something into the ear of the Empress.

"Oh!" she said. "What is the business of the day?"

"The first item," said the Consul, "is a message from the Sultan."

The Emperor did his best to show no change in his imperial demeanor. The Empress was gripping his wrist tightly, but otherwise remaining admirably cool.

"And what does our most loyal vassal have to say to us?" the Emperor asked.

The Consul unrolled an impressive scroll inscribed in the wonderfully ornate calligraphy of the Sultan's chancery:

" 'The Sultan to his most beneficent and fatherly lord the Emperor, prosperity. Our Sultanate rejoices as one man at the news of your happy nuptials, and we pray unceasingly to Apollyon to bring you joy and a multitude of heirs. May you and the Empress live forever in peace and wisdom.' "

The Consul rolled up the scroll. The Tribune sneezed.

The Emperor felt the Empress' grip relaxing. He himself could not keep a smile from poking through his imperial dignity. "We must send the Sultan a message of thanks."

"Don't you think we could send him a present of some sort?" the Empress suggested.

"We've been working on a present for his birthday," the Emperor said. "We send him one every year."

"But what about one besides that? Something special in honor of our wedding. A thing that would be, well, weddingy."

"We had a mosaic," said the Emperor. "It was...well, it had to do with love, anyway."

"Oh! Can I see it?"

"Consul," said the Emperor, "could we have that mosaic with the... the..."

The Consul filled in, "Amorous scenes from the ancient heathen mythology."

"Yes. Could that be brought?"

"Is it..." The Consul began to approach as he spoke in a more confidential tone, but Jerome growled, and the Consul decided to maintain his respectful distance. "Is it quite suitable for a lady?"

"It's got a lot of ladies in it," the Emperor pointed out; and since this was self-evidently true, the Consul made no more objection, but simply called for a messenger. The call bounced between the two rows of guards on the left and on the right, and in moments a messenger was running toward the throne. When he reached the front of the hall, he was given his instructions and sent off to the Master of the Treasury. Meanwhile the Tribune took the opportunity to sneeze.

"While we wait for the mosaic," said the Consul,

"with the permission of your clemency and your clemency, we may proceed to the other business of the day. Our general on the Aspersian front reports sound victories..."

And so the Empire continued. If there was no Aspersian war, there was at least news from the front, and that was the same thing. There might be no province of Lesser Occidens, but the Emperor dealt with the corruption in its administration just as if it existed. He was a prisoner of his perceptions, but he had a comfortable prison, and he had made it himself. He had chosen his own conditions: he had taken control of his fictional world.

And then the Master of the Treasury arrived, with his cart and four cart-pushers, and the Empress and the Emperor stepped down to examine the mosaic.

"Oh, how sweet!" the Empress exclaimed, and she began to subject the pictures to a minute examination. "This one... And this one..." And then she looked up. "Here's one we haven't tried."

"I don't think that one's physically possible," said the Emperor.

"Sure it is. I'll bet you anything." She returned to her close examination. "We might need some ropes and a pulley..." After some more close perusal, she asked, "Don't you think this would be perfect for the Sultan? With all those wives, he must be looking for suggestions."

"Consul," said the Emperor, "it is the will of the Empress that this mosaic be presented to the Sultan as a gift in honor of the imperial wedding."

The Consul bowed. "The will of the Empress is law," he said.

The Tribune sneezed, and Jerome roared his agreement.

CHAPTER 30

THE SULTAN'S COLLECTION

"GREAT and magnificent, O Sultan, is your collection," said the Maharajah, "and surely equaled by no other in the world. For we other poor collectors have been content with the rare material productions of the earth, but an Emperor with working miniature Empire is beyond not only our resources but even our imaginations."

Only etiquette prevented the Sultan's ministers from slapping each other on the back:—etiquette, and a lively sense of the ninety-cubit drop from the top of the Great Minaret of the Temple of Apollyon. From here the Sultan and his honored guest had a magnificent view of the palace across the Narrows to the west: the gardens and villas of the senatorial quarter on the shore in front, and the wonderfully immense Dome, the roof of the Hall of Lions, the smaller but still impressive dome of the Church of the Assumption, and high above everything else the Tower of Diotrephes, taller even than the Great Minaret, and standing on the highest point of the peninsula that made up the palace complex. The whole was set ablaze from behind by what would soon turn into a glorious sunset.

The Sultan's mustache had reached its broadest extent; but it contracted a little when the Maharajah spoke again.

"And yet it might be said that you do not entirely possess this Emperor or his Empire."

The Sultan's ministers stopped breathing for a moment, but the Sultan himself answered very mildly.

"Indeed, my dear Maharajah? And why night that be said?"

"Well, my dear Sultan, it seems that your pet Emperor has a will of his own, and a will, moreover, with which he has been able to defy yours. He did not, for example, marry your daughter."

"Oh, but my dear Maharajah, he *has* married my daughter."

"Indeed? It was my understanding that the men of his faith married but one wife. Has your Emperor converted to your own worship of Apollyon to marry Spring Blossom After the Rain as well?"

"No, my dear Maharajan, you misunderstand me. Pulcheria is my daughter."

The Maharajah's eyebrows rose considerably. "Your daughter? You did not mention that detail when you told me their story. Do you mean that she deceived your Emperor by disguising herself as a humble serving-girl?"

"She practiced no deception. She is not aware of her descent. But when the current Emperor was born, I determined that he should have a companion of his own choice. I also determined what that choice should be."

"How is that possible?" the Maharajah asked. "How could you determine his choice so far in advance?"

"Oh, it was a simple matter. An appropriate education

that instilled in him a longing to be his own man, so to speak; and from there it was an easy thing to make sure that the one young lady he met on his own was the right one, and nearly inevitable that everything should progress as I desired after that."

"So his ministers, the Consul and the Tribune—they were in fact working to bring the Emperor and Empress together?"

"No—no, they were unaware of my plans, and remain so."

"Yet you have not executed them for attempting to thwart your will?"

"Oh, no," said the Sultan. "Certainly not. It was essential that the Emperor should face and overcome strong opposition, so that he would feel the accomplishment as his own. Besides, they are much more amusing with their heads on than with their heads off, and what use is my collection if it does not amuse me?"

The sun had nearly reached the end of his course, and the sky was filled with red and salmon and gold. The palace across the strait was a dark filigree base for the wonderful display in the heavens.

"A magnificent collection indeed," said the Maharajah, and the Sultan's mustache reached maximum width again.

The Sultan's ministers did not smile, but it was clear that they were actively suppressing smiles.

"And yet," the Maharajah continued, "I almost pity that poor little man. The Emperor is living a life that he knows to be a lie. He cannot escape it, and the only thing he can do is submit to the lie and learn to find his pleasure in things he knows to be false."

The last sliver of sun disappeared behind the dome of the Church of the Assumption, but the celestial spectacle was only beginning.

"Do you know," said the Sultan, "I think that poor little man may be the only really happy man in the world."

Made in the USA
Middletown, DE
17 August 2022

70659820R00142